The Harboring

& other stories

Kathleen M. Jacobs

Jan-Carol
Publishing, Inc
"every story needs a book"

The Harboring & other stories
Kathleen M. Jacobs

First Edition Published June 2025
Little Creek Books
Imprint of Jan-Carol Publishing, Inc.
Cover Design: Tara Sizemore
Cover Photograph: Nadezhda/Adobe Stock
All rights reserved
Copyright © Kathleen M. Jacobs

ISBN: 978-1-962561-75-4
Library of Congress Control Number: 2025941564

You may contact the publisher:
Jan-Carol Publishing, Inc.
PO Box 701
Johnson City, TN 37605
publisher@jancarolpublishing.com
jancarolpublishing.com

For all women who find the strength to persevere,
define resiliency, embrace resolve, and blaze new paths.

Also by Kathleen M. Jacobs

Honeysuckle Holiday

Marble Town

Collected Curiosities: Poems, Essays, & Opinions

Please Close It!

The Puppeteer of Objects: A Lyrical Poem

Betsy Blossom Brown

Sophie & the Bookmobile

Fireflies Dancing in the Night

Author's Note

When my family moved from St. Louis to rural West Virginia when I was at a most impressionable age, I knew that my diary entries and my imagination would change. I just didn't know to what degree those changes would transform me over the years that followed. Most of the change was propelled by the invitation extended from the natural landscape of the forest floor, the heavy Appalachian dialect, and a roiling river that separated one mountain from another. The recent recognition of the New River Gorge as a National Park and Preserve tipped the scales to represent all good things in my world. It brought full circle all the youthful experiences that grew in intensity to experiences as a young adult and well into the years beyond. These experiences led to my penning one work after another, until they reached a crescendo with this work.

Every story in this collection has its roots in the resiliency of the Appalachian woman. They are as closely linked as swimming is to getting wet. This journey began with a most horrific murder in my hometown of Charleston, West Virginia, some years after the start of the twenty-first century. I knew both parties as well as I knew the parties that planted the seeds in each of these stories. And while I had initially seen the collection as a work of creative non-fiction (reminiscent of Truman Capote's *In Cold Blood*), it wasn't until the collection's completion that I began to see it not only as a testament to the resiliency of Appalachian women but to the resiliency of all women, with Appalachian women leading the way. Historically, Appalachian women have walked a very unsettled path on levels well known by all. As I told each story, what became so very clear were not just their perseverance and resiliency and resolve, but their self-respect to guard what was known about themselves and each other and the trust and respect that bound them, one to the other, through every traumatic and celebratory moment of their lives. Infusing their stories with a strong dose of imaginative details allowed me to protect not only their individual stories but to make certain that every reader recognized their own struggles, and that every story became a universal story.

The seeds of this collection were planted so very early on in my writing journey, growing in ways that I couldn't have possibly imagined. The journey has been both remarkable and surreal, finally setting me down a path that, without any early admission, answered the question posed by a most enlightened spiritual adviser, "Why do you think you relate on such a deep level with these women?" The answer, after years of hoping otherwise, became as clear as the rippling waters of the creek that first welcomed me to Appalachia so long ago.

Playlist

1. "Cat's in the Cradle" Eric Clapton
2. "Whole Lotta Love" Led Zeppelin
3. "Fly Me to the Moon" Frank Sinatra
4. "Letting Go" Hennie Bekker
5. "Take Me Home, Country Roads" Lana Del Rey
6. "Wake Me Up" Avicii
7. "Unstoppable" Sia
8. "Flowers" Miley Cyrus
9. "Stop Draggin' My Heart Around" Stevie Nicks, Tom Petty and the Heartbreakers
10. "Respect" Aretha Franklin
11. "I Will Survive" Gloria Gaynor

A wise woman builds her house, while a foolish woman tears hers down with her own hands.

— Proverbs 14:1

I would rather sit on a pumpkin and have it all to myself, than be crowded on a velvet cushion.

— Henry David Thoreau

The Harboring

For there is nothing covered up that will not be revealed, nor hidden that will not be known. Therefore whatever you have spoken in the dark will be heard in the light, and what you have spoken in the ear in inner rooms will be proclaimed on the housetops. — LUKE 12:2-3

One

The crumbling white clapboard house on Crow Creek Road had recently been condemned and was scheduled for demolition one week from today. Remains of pale yellow and grass green exterior paint from too long ago to recall popped up in patches around the house, in an unidentifiable pattern, reminiscent of a Rorschach test.

Not even the land on which it stood was worth much of anything; it was a mystery how the house had remained standing for as long as it had. Not much thought was given by anyone as to when the construction of the house began, but from all appearances it could be surmised that the 1940s was as good a guess as any. The house sat on a slight knoll with a gravel road on one side, and on the other a soggy, sloping yard that was perched precariously close to the creek that was known to rise without much warning whenever heavy rains caused the waters to rush over the protruding, solid, jagged boulders that had been there longer than the house.

Basement floors in this part of the state particularly were most always unusable, even for storage, with a continual, yet barely visible, fine stream of water seeping from the cracked, settled foundation. A few makeshift metal shelves had been secured to the moldy sheetrock that had been used to store Ball jars that held preserves and pickles and sweet peppers, all of which could be seen from the highway through the bare window openings, whose glass panes had long ago been obliterated by vandals.

The varying shades of green and red brought to mind the Christmas season even on the most humid of Appalachian summer days. Residents in this rapidly declining region with houses that had partial or full basements that had been built near its creeks accepted—without much of a fight—the fact that they would have to contend with a bit of water intrusion in their basements, installing everything from affordable dehumidifiers to complex systems designed to prevent such unwanted invasion, none of which ever seemed to work to alleviate the problem. Approaching the cascading waters along the rural roadway was a prelude to the appearance—seemingly out of nowhere and out of place—of the decaying structure that seemed content in its preserved state of decline. If it could speak, it would say how resigned it was to its imminent demise, assuming human qualities to dismiss any intruders who might, for unexplainable reasons, insist that it could indeed be brought back to life, like an episode from a home improvement television show.

The house had sat vacant for longer than anyone could remember, except maybe for Tommy, whose heart held fond childhood memories of time spent there and into his young adult years. Driving past the house on a narrow, two-lane, winding West Virginia road that led past the thick foliage of mountain laurel and rushing creek waters that met the jagged boulders that sat on the surface of the commanding New River made the dilapidated house nearly insignificant. And yet, amateur and professional photographers both known and unknown to the area parked their cars and trucks and vans in an open field not but a stone's throw from the house and walked the back road that led to the front of the house to click camera lenses, knowing that the journey was much too treacherous to make their way to the creek side of the house.

More than a few attempted to gain a footing on the slippery slope, but knowing that there was nowhere to go but into the uncertain waters, they retreated. It was at that moment that the self-imposed isolation of the house came to life, snickering as they walked away from what they couldn't conquer. The house had belonged to Tommy's paternal grandparents; his grandfather having built it plank by plank and brick by brick. Tommy would often speak of those times, attaching memories to them that may or may not have ever materialized, as over time the details of his recollections became varied enough that no listener called any discrepancies in the details to his attention. After all, what did any of it really matter at this point? These moments always brought to mind the Japanese phrase, *shiyou ga nai*, which had been shared years ago by a foreign exchange student from high school. What we want to remember is often embellished, either knowingly or not. And if there is no harm in remembering what we want to remember rather than remembering the sometimes painful reality, then we shrug our shoulders and move on, supporting each other's pretensions with complete conviction at the time that there is no harmful seed being dropped into an early, shallow grave.

About an hour's drive west of Crow Creek Road is a city that sits at the confluence of the Elk and Kanawha rivers. It is mistaken as a small big city; when, in fact, it is a big small town. For reasons I've yet to determine, this realization is met with an unsettling defensiveness that is deeply embedded. It has been my home since I was born, and it was my parents' and grandparents' home before that, with aunts and uncles and cousins and friends and acquaintances all within a few miles of one another. I rather like that it's a big, small town rather than a small, big city, but I've learned to keep that endearment to myself.

Tommy's heritage mimicked mine, as did that of most families in the state—the only state that is technically entirely Appalachian. It was a source of pride and, at times, a source of deep concern and deep frustration with our intentional refusal to change, even if we had all wanted to. Most of us chose the side of pride, refusing to consider the role conditioning played in each of our lives. It was less consuming.

And I—nor any of those I knew—never gave much thought to leaving, and when we did, it was a fleeting trip, except for the few times we all traveled as if moved by some religious cult to Myrtle Beach on holiday or business trips throughout the region, with an occasional trip abroad. And for reasons unaccounted for, Canada was not considered abroad by anyone I had ever talked with. Europe, yes. Canada, no. Again, any dedicated time to wondering about this unusual attitude was quickly filed away.

I once tagged along with my husband when he traveled to London for business. I say "tagged along," because that's what I always felt like whenever he and I went anywhere together. It's not that he walked in front of me—or behind me, for that matter—but that I never really felt that we were one, a deeply resonate proclamation and indisputable truth that was delivered with such an undeniable conviction at mass on our wedding day that I was certain the thunder that was gathering outside roared. It was an autumnal day that had started with a steady, cool trickle of rain that grew into a major thunderstorm, enduring well into the evening. It was a day that now seems like such a long time ago. And then sometimes, it seems as if it happened just yesterday. But I know it didn't. It was a long time ago. And while I never thought we'd both stay in Charleston after the divorce, we did. And the awkward nature of this choice became unexpectedly irrelevant.

And for the past five years, he (I always refer to him as "he" rather than by his name—it helps to pretend, which even I know isn't a smart thing to do) and I barely acknowledge each other whenever our paths happen to cross, which, thankfully and surprisingly for a city the size of Charleston, seldom happens. But I do it anyway—refer to him as someone without a name. It's a little game I play with myself. After all, who knows besides me? And sometimes I find myself giggling at the immaturity of it, and yet I giggle nonetheless, glancing around me to see if anyone has noticed, much like a small child caught in the act. And there are days when I feel just like that—a small, unknowing child waiting with an uneasy but certain expectancy at what lies ahead. And now, as I reflect on the events that led me to finally accept Tommy's invitation to take a ride with him after work to walk around his grandparents' house one last time before it was demolished, I'm a bit flushed, recalling the moment I said, "Why not?"

He had asked numerous times before, and I'd always said, "No, I don't think so, but thanks." As far as I know, I wasn't being coy. And if so, it was unintentional. And every time I rejected him, he would look away, sending his chin-length auburn wavy hair behind each ear, looking down until a customer walked towards the shoe department of Bailey & Sons Outfitters, and the ritual of making certain his shirt was tucked in would begin. His starched, white, button-down Oxford dress shirt was always tucked securely inside his perfectly creased trousers. And every time he did this, I recited, silently of course, Jane Kenyon's poem, "The Shirt," that I had memorized long ago and have never forgotten, visualizing the slow, certain journey of the shirt's tail, feeling the heat rise on my neck, looking—once again—to see if anyone had noticed my hypocrisy, even as I was quick to deny it myself. Then he would straighten the gold-tone horseshoe buckle of his black leather belt, smooth down his pressed, black dress trousers, and look at the cuffs that barely graced the tassels on his polished, cordovan loafers.

I imagined him a bit like a doll on a metal stand, and my hours of dressing and undressing my Ken doll returned to me in vivid detail. Once again, I turned away, but this time with unwelcome shame, not sure if it was related to desire or disgust. And with that thought, I couldn't help but wonder if he saw me the same way—two seemingly animate objects living our lives as if we were anything but, as if the end had already come and gone and we were bystanders gazing, along with all the others, at the incredulity of what had happened.

The buildup of this evening's carefully choreographed events is the result of the past year's increasing flirtations with one another (oh, how sophomoric that sounds!), as if all our other possibilities are either married or are in long-term relationships and, because of my own failed marriage and Tommy's fierce attachment to remaining single, we know that we are what's available for each other right now. And lately, as knowingly pathetic as that all seems, it has been enough. And we both know this, without ever vocalizing it—this heavy desperation, this hunger that gnaws at each of us. It is so stifling that I loosen the knotted silk scarf at my throat in order to exhale with less exertion. Without saying it, we are what the other has as a possible dating option, albeit one that doesn't necessarily hold much passion for either of us. Even the word "dating," in our case, is absurd. We're like the last people chosen on the playground for a softball team, and we each know this, too. And the desperation is a silent one, knowing it of ourselves and of each other but guarding it as if our lives depended on it, as if the acceptance of its very engagement would surely lead to our respective ends, which in reality is the stage that has been set with such exact precision. And in that quiet, mutual acknowledgment, there is a bond that, while neither of us particularly likes it, we understand it—a bond that is binding whether we want it to be or not.

And there is something so frightening about that acknowledgment that the gentle but certain trembling of my body has covered me without any warning, like a slow, steady rain; the thunder making its own plans. And while this growing urgency to accept the inevitable builds, the meticulously planned also reminds me that even though I will witness the leveling of Tommy's grandparents' house, I am also fully aware of my own certain demise, which I find comforting. And as the appointed time's momentum builds, I find too that I am as gleeful as a child waking on Christmas morning. This acknowledgment has elevated my adrenaline level well past anything I've ever imagined or experienced. It is sensual in a way that it shouldn't be—should never be. And very much like a sleepwalker, I stroll through the imaginary, but for me, very real door to what awaits and beckons beyond.

Two

As the morning made its way to early afternoon, I was overcome with a pressing certainty that I wanted to fill the few hours remaining before that defining moment with the overabundance of beauty that only nature could promise. Driving north, I parked in an all-too-familiar spot at the top of the hill in the center of a park where I had spent so much of my youth and my early years with a husband with whom I thought I'd grow old, only to be dropped as if from its highest point to the vast ravine below.

The spot was just a short distance from a mammoth, jagged cliff that resembled the inside of a cocoon. I exited the car, embraced the warm breeze, and began a walk I've treaded gently more times than I can remember. I find everything fully alive, as I bid each familiar one goodbye: a slithering garden snake making its way through the brambles, a hypnotic slant of sunlight, a leaping frog, a bumble bee flitting about for nectar, a spattering of mustard-colored paint on a tree's rugged trunk, the underbelly of a leaf, a ladybug resting on a soft mound of pin cushion moss, and a turtle meandering across what to him must be an exaggerated length of roadway to get from one side to the other. I stop briefly beside a blossoming, intricately interwoven honeysuckle hedge, close my eyes, inhale deeply, and exhale slowly.

I pull from its branches a full blossom and extract from it all it has to give. I tuck its barren petals behind my ear, open wide my arms, and look to the bright blue sky, in awe of its too-many-to-count puffy, white clouds, as if to say, "I'm on my way. Hold a spot for me, one of your least deserving, but one of your oh, so very expectant."

I return to my car, start the engine, and make my descent.

Three

Tommy enjoyed a reputation of flirting with anyone who wore a skirt, and everyone knew that if I saw my husband with his new wife and their Gerber-like twins one more time, I'd likely snap. Part of the reason we divorced was because I couldn't get pregnant, and we tried everything. I didn't think it mattered as much as it did to him, because I hadn't married him in order to conceive and raise children, but because I was deeply in love with him. But after a few years of failed attempts, his irritability grew and mine eventually caught up.

Soon, we were spending more time alone than together. And somewhere along the way, he fell in love with someone who gave him twins. And that was it. The happily-ever-after life I had imagined died a not-so-slow death, and for the past five years I've felt as if I've been floating on a cloud, looking down on his life with his new wife and their Gerber-like offspring. It's unnerving, but there is also an attractive, delusional quality to it, not unlike the effects of a hallucinogen, which I've heard about but never experienced. And there I go again, making certain that my deeply embedded Catholic girl-can-do-no-wrong reputation remains untainted and transparent, as I yearn to be anything but, to plunge into the deep end of the pool and do something so uncharacteristic that it surprises even me. And perhaps it is that recurring thought that caused me to grow more certain of accepting Tommy's invitation, turning that lifelong, goody-two-shoes, nearly repulsive reputation on its shaky axis.

After all, I have been moving in that direction for the past several years. And there is something alluring in the notion of change. And Tommy must sense it too, because he's just made eye contact and nodded, a faint smile trying hard to emerge, along with that intoxicating wink that if I could somehow control just might save both of us from the inevitable. And I turn from him as if he can read my thoughts, which are slightly more than daring, and yet I imagine not unlike his own, as each of us continues to inch closer and closer to revealing our core, like peeling back one layer at a time the thin, papery skin of an onion.

I could have moved out of town and started a new life somewhere far away from my husband, but who does that when their entire family and social circle—regardless of number—lives within a few miles of one another? Obviously not me, even though I imagined what my life would be like if I registered on a dating site and moved my meager belongings with me in my Volvo C30, taking with me my equally meager trust account. I often flipped through the pages of *Travel* magazine, imagining myself in La Jolla, or New York City, or the coast of Maine, or even the middle of Iowa, meeting and falling in love with a farmer who produced row after row of corn every year and who would pick me up and sit me right down beside him as he plowed the fields, not necessarily ever giving thought to a brood of offspring.

I didn't know of many farmers, and the ones I did know had a gaggle of geese, so to speak. And every single time, I ended up tossing the magazine into the trash and falling into my nightly routine of taking a shower and brushing my teeth and applying a much-too-liberal amount of moisturizer before burying myself underneath a mountain of quilts, the portable DVD player on the nightstand putting me to sleep with the sounds from *October Sky*, which I have seen so many times I don't even need to watch or listen any longer, because I can recite the entire script without much prompting. And while I most closely resemble Homer's innocent, shy girlfriend, Valentine, it was Dorothy who I most wanted to be like—who inside I felt most comfortable, most alluring, most exciting, and yet a part that never saw the light of day. A part that I'm recognizing is beginning to emerge more fully than ever before—at least in my mind, if nowhere else. And that thought both frightens me and excites me.

And now, this evening, I feel that she might bring herself out of the shadows and into the full light of the moon. I could almost hear the creaking sounds from the rusted door hinge at the house on Crow Creek Road opening an inch at a time, hesitating to open wide to reveal all that had been kept hidden, simmering over a low flame for longer than humanly bearable. And it is the creaking sounds that are becoming most inviting, most hypnotic. And I find this admission both unsettling and inexplicable.

In my ruminations, I looked to Tommy's desk to glance at the photograph of his grandparents' house from the back of the property that always sat there, as if glued to the thin plywood. The rush of the creek, while still in the photograph, seemed to eerily move whenever I looked at it, like the picture of Jesus Christ that hung in my own grandparents' house when I was a child; Jesus's eyes seeming to follow me wherever I went. It frightened me then, and it frightens me still—even as a memory. And while the humidity outside on this stifling hot August afternoon nears 100 percent, I am suddenly chilled from head to toe. I bring my arms up and around me as if to wrap myself from what I do not know; yet I somehow know—instinctively know—that I need protection, but uncertain as to the reason and completely resistant to it, regardless of its promised fatalism.

As I reach a near-hypnotic state from staring deep into the photograph, as if trying to see inside the house, walking precariously from one room to the other while my imagination runs away from me, what I notice is the organic overgrowth of vegetation, the green acutely emerald, and I am transported to the Emerald City of Oz hoping for a chance to meet with the Wizard and then just as quickly hoping that he's unavailable. Perhaps he'll dismiss me with little effort, telling me to return another day—or never. And the luster fades almost immediately, as the overgrowth appears to wind its way around every tree trunk, across every blade of grass and through every opened window of the decaying white clapboard house, an exterior white that has chipped and cracked and peeled over time, like the tapped shell of a hard-boiled egg. An exterior that has grown the color of mantis green that no amount of power washing could erase.

The moss that has formed in patches on the roof's top looks like lush, padded stepping stones, and I want to frolic from one to the other, with the ease reserved only for childhood. Instead, I realize that I have been holding my breath, feeling as if the vines that weave their way in and out of the decaying house are cutting off not only the life of the house and those who once lived there, but my very own oxygen, and the immense exhale that escapes is both welcomed and haunting. As I look closer, a bit of the dirt and gravel road at the front of the house is barely visible, with a meandering mountain on the far side. The old shingle roof slopes here and there, and pieces of the bricks from the decaying chimney are scattered about like a handful of jacks. A flock of birds is poised at the top, with one waiting to dive deep into its cavernous opening. The rusted gutters hang on—by what I'm not sure, but they appear to dangle, like Christmas ornaments from a tree, even though I know I'm imagining.

The English ivy has built a wall between the two back, bare windows, and I wonder how long the house has sat with nothing but nature's own adornments. The overhang of trees creates a canopy as if one simple pebble hurled at it could collapse and erase its entire history. And Edgar Allan Poe's "The Fall of the House of Usher" is more than clear in my mind. I yearn to see the front of the house; the one that faces away from me, the one that meets the gravel road. In the distance, I notice a tree trunk with a handmade sign that reads, DO NOT DISTURB, the crude drawing of a slithering snake winding its way between each letter, its opened mouth beginning to absorb the final one. And with an equal urgency, I want desperately to know why Tommy has changed the photograph in the frame to show the house in its current decay rather than the one from his childhood that held memories of summer nights chasing fireflies and roasting marshmallows, holiday celebrations, and family gatherings throughout the years—much like my own. A house void of its current decay. A house vibrant with the sights and sounds and tastes of everyday life, even with its ups and downs and losses and disappointments.

And in wondering why he has chosen to change out the photographs, I try without success to pinpoint the day when the photograph changed. And why hadn't I noticed it before? Why would he choose to display a photograph of a decaying house without any fond memories? And at that precise recognition and without really knowing why, I am more certain than ever that seeing this evening through to completion will be the most defining moment of my life. It's a decision whose certainty is made without a single regret. I am aware that the option to reverse my decision is set before me like a colorful macaron on a delicately painted fine China dessert plate, and yet I find myself powerless to say, "No." I am suddenly overcome with the desire to see the other side of the house and the road that will take me there. With cautious anxiety, I whisper, "Yes," once again, to hear its unfamiliar, yet so very easy, notes; to see if the sound of assent unsettles me. I am comforted that it doesn't.

I feel an equally unfamiliar grin emerge as I keep straight my head and look only with my peripheral vision, knowing that the journey has already begun—a journey that comes not with a delightful dream, but only with the sharp focus of a terrifying nightmare, yet one I'm pulled into by a force other than my own. And that's the moment I lock eyes with Tommy, and he knows too what I already imagine, his slight grin matching mine, as if there had never been a doubt in his mind, not certain how long he has watched me dissect the harrowing photograph on his desk.

Four

Beautifully appointed one bedroom, one bath, detached, newly constructed apartment in the city's historic east end district. Eateries, shops, and capitol grounds all within walking distance, along with the city's new, indoor farmers' market. The third-floor rooftop terrace is perfect for reading, relaxing, and entertaining small gatherings.

After the divorce, I left the historic, early 1800s Federal-style house I shared with my husband in the eastern part of the county. After the wedding, he used part of the first floor as his law office, until his practice grew rapidly, causing him to lease space in an imposing downtown bank building. The house's two-story brick exterior was painted a glaring white. While indeed stately, its high gloss cherry red front door stood as a much too-emboldened attraction for me; and yet, it remained. The door's heavy brass, tarnished wolf doorknocker was a sign of the silent, yet emotionally charged lives that were being led just inside. And it was the silence of its caretakers that was most destructive to my core. I learned early on that silence can be deafening, and I often covered my ears in mute revolt.

It sat on two acres of level land, with a carpet of green the color of a shamrock. I often found that comparison more than a bit hypocritical. And yet, it remained a constant, much like everything else. And, much like everything else, it wasn't discussed. Unrest—real or imagined—was avoided as much as the color of the main door or the imposing doorknocker that became the albatross whose weight I carried, without questioning. The interior's exposed brick walls and wide plank hickory floors and elaborate, intricately carved mantels and fireplace surrounds and built-in bookcases that flanked each fireplace in all the bedrooms and the living room and the formal dining room appealed to my attraction to symmetry.

The exterior's design resembled the Federal style, typically presented as a square or rectangular box, with subtle classical detailing. Its elliptical-arched main entrance was impressive and beautifully understated; its etched glass with side slender windows, mysteriously inviting. Four long, slender windows were meticulously placed, one on top of the other, in pairs, with unbridled precision at each level and at each half. At the top center, above the main entrance, was a nook that I claimed for myself; one that seemed to invite the stories I wanted to write, did write, but never shared with anyone. All the interior furnishings had been left by the previous owners, whose millennial heirs' only interest was monetary, rather than the preservation of the sacrifices and rewards that history records. The finely woven Aubusson rugs throughout the house, the oil paintings of ancestors that graced every wall, the four-poster mahogany beds, and even the early works of classical literature were all left behind.

Even the early American flag that waved from the front of the house and the heavily upholstered wingback chairs and camelback sofas and the massive cherry wardrobes had been orphaned. Rich chocolate-brown, worn leather captain's chairs and threadbare needle-pointed dining chairs and shimmering chandeliers showed unhappy signs of being left behind, expectant that we would hold them sacred enough that they hadn't felt completely abandoned. The black and white penny tile on the master bath floor and the built-in linen press brought joy every time I reached inside for fresh linens—the aroma of time past and cedar and a bit of pipe tobacco emanating from its corners. I often wished I could light the scent as if from a candle's wick. The hand-wrought iron interior door bolts and original screws and locks with their skeleton keys and dull, but handsome, worn smooth knobs seemed to speak to me in a language that no one else could understand. And every time I walked by one, I smiled, and it seemed to smile back at me, reverting to its unassuming glance once I passed.

The back of the main house leading out from the sparsely equipped kitchen included a door that was painted the color of corn. A few steps out, a dwelling in a near-replication of the main house was most alluring to me in its decrepit state and a bit cultish in its seduction. It was too raw, too primitive for habitation, but I longed to restore it and lock myself away from what I couldn't escape in a marriage that I never—even from the beginning—felt fully immersed in. Throughout the unhurried days, listening to the rhythm of the handsome grandfather clock in the front entry, I would roam from room to room, knowing not to disturb anything, for he would notice upon arrival and, without hesitation, return whatever had been disturbed to its original place. And I, with a degree of submissiveness that I found intolerable, said nothing. And while that reticence was never surprising to me, for I had witnessed it my whole life from those whose married years numbered in the decades, I longed to live out the stories that I had written of being set free from the shackles that I had imposed upon myself, looking everywhere for the keys that would unlock them all, not knowing that all along I kept them buried deep in my pocket.

To even entertain the thought of the dissolution of our marriage would require something so harrowing to take place that even I, as a writer of stories based on vivid imaginings could not have conjured. And yet, nearly five years later, Mother Nature had intervened, and I hadn't yet decided if I had secretly welcomed her or if she had sensed the inevitable, silently agreeing to act as an objective interloper.

Sliding open the drawer to my desk, I read again a poem that I had penned not long after our arrival, sliding it back inside the drawer, and closing it gently—"The Pink Velvet Sofa": *Anchored by a worn Aubusson rug, it held my secrets. The far left corner, opposite my perch, my darkest. Moments abandoned, moments lost to ignorance, betrayals. Claw-footed legs left deep impressions, time their only savior. Turning the faded Aubusson one-eighty would serve no purpose, save to mask disarming truths, now secure underfoot, no longer as blinding.*

Five

lthough the monthly lease was above my intended budget, I
made the phone call before someone else could secure the
apartment. The owner was a law partner of my husband's,
and there was a certain degree of satisfaction in my efforts to forge
ahead on my own, even though loneliness had already wiggled its
way into every crevice of my body. As much as our home had an
over-abundance of character and grace and history, The Harboring's
exterior was as cold as I felt on even the most sultry of summer days.

Reclaimed materials of steel and weathered copper blinded me in
the direct sunlight, but the four floor-to-ceiling windows across the
building's front opened my world to what lay across the street: the
frolicking children that ran from one end of the playground to the
other, laughing, singing, and even sparring with one another. The
city's only Montessori School was directly in front of me as I propped
my feet up on a bright fuchsia-colored pouf ottoman in a heavy cotton.
I sat in front of it in a mid-century modern chair with a checkered
pattern in shades of brown. Both were anchored by an indoor-outdoor
woven cotton striped white and lime green rug. I found the chatter of
children both agonizing and comforting, unable to discern why.

The Harboring was a three-story building. The front entrance
boasted a pair of heavy, reclaimed double doors that once secured the

city's only Catholic church. Once inside, there was a small laundry room and a wooden strip with metal hooks attached to the wall for outerwear. Ascending the narrow, winding stairs covered in a light birch wood floor, I always stopped to gaze out of the single window, whose view was nearly flush with the window. The magnificent magnolia leaves, when in bloom, arrested me and kept me planted firmly on the narrow landing, until there was nothing left to do but climb the few remaining stairs to the second floor living area, kitchen and sparkling bath, awash in gray marble tiled floors. The kitchen offered a line-up of reclaimed steel cabinets and slate countertops, none of which I used very often. I had enough of the essentials to accomplish what needed accomplished, but my needs were meager: oatmeal for breakfast with an apple and a piece of toasted raisin-cinnamon bread; goat cheese with blueberries and crackers for lunch; and more often than not penne pasta with a bit of storebought marinara sauce for dinner. It was enough nourishment for my body—not near enough for my spirit, which I knew was beginning to decline in a fashion that I couldn't stop. And maybe I didn't want to stop.

Retiring to the third-floor bedroom's wooden platform bed with a slim mattress became so disruptive to my sense of self that I, instead, often slept on an inflated mattress on the second floor. While it proved a bit awkward entering and exiting, the alternative was enough for me to make the necessary accommodations. The first few years, I budgeted my meager allowances, making certain that I did not put myself in a situation where I would have to depend on securing employment; and yet, the time passed at an agonizingly slow pace. I often walked to the public library, checking out more self-help books than I cared to read, mainstream fiction that was as predictable as my daily routine, eventually revisiting childhood favorites, until they so deeply piqued my renewed attraction to them that I began to write stories for young readers, using stack after stack of lined notebook paper that I picked up for little to nothing at a family-owned discount store a few blocks from my apartment.

I kept my world small, intentionally. I seldom left the apartment, and the owner, who lived in the house directly behind The Harboring, was often out of town. My days ran one into the other until I couldn't tell them apart, except for the weekends when the Montessori school was closed. Those two days lingered in a decaying way, like a too-ripe, shriveled peach. When a neighbor stopped me on an early spring morning walk when the dogwoods were in full bloom along both sides of the street, mentioning that Bailey & Sons Outfitters was looking to hire a salesperson for their line of women's fashions, my interest was piqued enough to give them a call the next day. My husband had shopped there, as did his father and anybody who was anybody in town. I knew that I didn't want to work every day, but I also knew that if I didn't secure something outside these four walls that I would sink farther into a hole that had become much deeper than I had ever imagined.

While tempted to continue on my path to total isolation, I unearthed enough of a desire to live a fuller life from some deep reservoir within myself. After the interview with the store's owner, I was offered a position working a few days a week, with the potential to move into a full-time position. I did not share that I would not consider a full-time position. That, I kept to myself. After the divorce, I made the immutable decision to never again put myself in a position where I was not in complete control. And while I was still on shaky ground, I knew that much to be true. I knew I would not compromise that position ever again.

Six

Bailey & Sons has stylishly outfitted discerning men and women of the area for generations, providing classic, timeless fashions for professionals and fashion-conscious members of society.

And that creed is not only deeply embedded into each and every sales associate at Bailey & Sons, but it is indeed etched on the glass underneath the indigo Bailey & Sons storefront window, along with an image of an impeccably dressed gentleman and lady, each carrying a leather briefcase, with more than one youngster trailing behind. Even then, Bailey & Sons impressed upon its clientele the importance of family—long before that priority was relegated to a much lesser importance, becoming nearly obsolete with the dawn of the new millennium and the emergence and acceptance of self-absorption took its place. To secure a position as a sales associate/fashion consultant with Bailey & Sons required more than mere pedigree.

A certain sense of style, an impeccable reputation, and a stellar standing in the community all play a significant role with the HR department, headed by a Bailey who has taken the helm generation after generation into the next generation. Staff had included graduates from colleges who majored in fashion design and business and accounting as well as fashion merchandising. Summer interns are gathered from esteemed clients and treasured employees, whose tenure more often than not runs into decades of service. But it is the coveted Bailey & Sons breast pin that each employee is given to wear while in service to its clients that brings it all full circle, the indigo script matching the storefront's window, a cinched pair of white gloves underneath. The solid wood door, with its heavy, seasoned brass fox door knocker at the side entrance for employees guides each one to the full-length mirror that has stood inside the door since it was placed there by Douglas Bailey when the store opened in 1935. He received it as a gift from his father, who had longed to open a men's clothing store that catered to the city's growing number of lawyers and doctors, entrepreneurs and coal magnates.

Its original purpose was to serve as a checkpoint for employees to remind them to take a look at themselves before clocking in for the day. Etched at the top of the mirror—now barely discernible—are the words: *Head to Toe, Side to Side, & Front to Back—Nothing Lacked. SMILE.* And below the last word was an etched smile as broad as a circus clown's. And while more than one employee longed to add a bit of their own words and images to the mirror, it never surfaced except in morning conversation or after-work banter.

A few days after I began my tenure at Bailey & Sons, I met Tommy. Several weeks later, he invited me to join him for a hotdog at his uncle's bar and grill across the street. Mike's Dogs & Fries had been in business almost as long as Bailey & Sons, passing the baton from one generation to the next in a city that had grown into that forged chain of each generation moving seamlessly from one to the next. It was the homemade chili that brought people in by the dozens every day. That and the show that Mike performed, lining up steamed hotdog buns from inside his wrist to his elbow with precision, placing first the boiled hotdog, the squiggly stream of yellow mustard, the revered chili, and finally a mound of creamy coleslaw, chopped onions throughout. And as he delivered each one to a plate filled with hand-cut fries and a dill pickle spear, cheers erupted at the line of barstools, the backdrop an elaborately carved massive oak bar brought over from France. It too graced an equally massive etched mirror with *Mike's Dogs & Fries* in heavy cursive, a steaming hotdog in a bun with all the toppings taking center stage below it.

Tommy and I sat at the counter gathering clean the toppings that fell to the white plate, leaving without ever paying a tab, never receiving a tab, for Tommy's uncle wouldn't hear of it. "You're family," he'd bellow, wiping his mustard-stained fingers across his soiled apron. "Thanks, Uncle Mike," Tommy would echo, and then Mike would wink at me as if he was certain that the day would arrive when payment would indeed be collected—something else that had caught on like the measles, identifying the city with a certain *je ne sais quoi* that flowed through the thickest of blood, without definition yet knowing full well the bill would eventually come due. And it never occurred to anyone to do anything about it or to simply reject it. And it was at those moments that I told myself that I'd not return to Mike's Dogs & Fries, yet I found myself returning time and again, perhaps because there was some intrigue that drew me there, as if I had sleepwalked across the street on someone else's accord.

"Tommy!" Lloyd Crouse bellowed, as he slapped Tommy's back. Whenever Senator Crouse came into the store, Tommy seemed to always set firm his stance, knowing that the state senator from our district would slap him on his back as if Tommy were a fellow football player on a college football team.

Where Senator Crouse was loud and boisterous and much-too-demonstrative in his greeting, Tommy was just the opposite. He was often reticent, always keenly observant, and at times caught in what seemed to be a trance, a dead stare fixed on a point only he knew. It was at those times that I felt a closeness to Tommy that startled me more than a little. His reflective nature seemed almost magical, even though there was an eeriness to it that I could never quite figure out. And yet it was that very mysterious eeriness that drew me to him, even though it wasn't something I consciously did. It was as if there was another me acting on impulse—an impulse that I had never before acted on. Another me that slid with ease from my core that longed to explore the unfamiliar, the uncertain, the dangerous part of my spirit—a spirit that had been in hibernation for far too many years. And there was something so inviting about it that a trance somewhat similar to the one Tommy engaged in also had me under its spell. And I think Tommy knew that, and he acted on it in a most unassuming, subtle way that I never knew about, until I did. And by then, it was too late.

"Good afternoon, Senator," Tommy said as he extended his arm to shake hands. The smile he offered Senator Crouse was the smile he reserved for all his clients: a forced attempt that only he knew came with a small dose—or perhaps more than a small amount—of feigned respect. "How may I assist you this morning, Senator?" Tommy continued, knowing that the senator liked the limelight—liked to dominate the conversation, asking questions that required very certain, abrupt answers that were sure to meet with agreement.

The senator had a penchant for shoes that matched his penchant for overindulgence. It was not a secret that he kept a shoe closet at his residence, located a few blocks west of the state capitol, on Kanawha Boulevard, overlooking the wide expanse of the Kanawha River. And it was no secret among the staff that his account was often past due and often over his generous limit and reluctantly tolerated because he and the senior Bailey had been fraternity brothers. And today, after he purchased a stack of shoes ranging from wingtips to athletic and a pair of pointed-toe cowboy boots, and a pair of house slippers, and several pairs of Sperrys to add to his seemingly endless collection, Tommy glanced at me as I gift-wrapped a cerulean cashmere sweater for the senator to give to his mistress of the past 25 years—an affair that was anything but secret, with the full knowledge of the senator's wife, who enjoyed her own dalliances.

As Senator Crouse turned to collect the sweater, Tommy tapped his wristwatch and winked. Even though I had tried to keep our lunch outings to a minimum, they became regular. They became certain. I smiled, knowing that it would not be long before the moment arrived when Tommy would leave his black, high-polished Corvette with cherry red leather interior in his parking space and settle himself in the passenger seat of my silver Volvo C30, and together we would head east to a place that really had no name—a place in between Chimney Corner and Fayetteville, and the last place that I'd ever travel with Tommy again. And even in the knowing, I knew I would go anyway. And there was something so frighteningly calming about the going that I didn't give much thought to what might happen when we arrived, knowing that I had imagined every step of the journey all along, as had Tommy. Two people not really knowing each other and yet knowing all that was needed to know.

Seven

It wasn't until 30 years after Bailey & Sons opened that it began to offer stylish fashions for women. Bailey senior's oldest son, Jack, was the only son to marry, and his new wife, Ellen, suggested the addition with enough conviction to convince Jack Senior to complement the store by offering a limited line of meticulously tailored suiting for women. Ellen naturally chose the finest fabrics: silk, cashmere, linen, and Pima cotton. The suiting was limited to business navy and black blazers with high-polished brass crested buttons and pencil skirts. Solid shirting was offered in white, baby blue, and pale pink, with two additional choices: a navy windowpane and a crimson stripe. A variety of silk scarves and cashmere sweaters in a rainbow of colors were neatly stacked inside the sleek cherry wood shelves behind the glass-front cases filled with men's shirts and sweaters and suspenders and linen handkerchiefs.

Walking through the double glass doors of Bailey & Sons, the scalloped skirt of its hunter green, heavy canvas awning blowing in the light breeze of an early morning start, the shine from its brass door handles blinding in the fresh sunlight, brought into view the parquet floor with its inset of a detailed compass. On either side of the center aisle, where outerwear hung from heavy, wooden hangers with the store's name and insignia impressed at the center, was gleaming cherry wood shelving, stacked perfectly with row after row of fine Pima cotton, solid-colored men's shirting and myriad choices of patterned selections. Fine cashmere sweaters were precisely folded and stacked, and one section held a small, but very coveted grouping of men's silk, flannel, and Pima cotton pajamas.

In front of the shelving units were gleaming glass cases filled with a sundry of accessories: kid leather gloves, silk pocket scarves, socks—both patterned and solid and athletic—undershirts and boxers and briefs, novelty and classic cufflinks, men's sock garters and suspenders, and starched stacks of linen and Pima cotton handkerchiefs—both novelty and classic; my favorite a blue and white gingham with a small embroidered snare drum, in the lower, right corner. Displayed on top of the glass cases—on both sides of the store—were circular racks of ties, in every imaginable color and pattern and style, with bowties holding court in separated slots of a rich, deep walnut wooden compartment. And at the center of the store sat a regal, gold-edged, deep cherry red table with fabric samples for custom shirting and suiting.

And fanning the stack of choices became a favored pastime for every associate, allured by the trance the simple action created. And as clients walked farther into the store, the center held a bevy of associates who, as if on regimented cue, welcomed everyone with the ease and informal formality that made everyone think they were the favored client. And that's the only way Bailey & Sons would have it. No exceptions. Each associate's dress was impeccable, with every hair in place, every shoe polished to a high sheen, and every smile seemingly genuine, regardless of what had happened in their respective lives that very morning. No hems raveled, no stains smeared, and no safety pins holding anything in place—at least not in clear sight. Beyond the center area, where in-house accounts were meticulously kept and guarded by a stern bookkeeper whose round, gold-rimmed spectacles were so firmly planted on the bridge of her nose that she was never, ever questioned—and she was never, ever wrong—was the men's shoe department on the right.

It too matched the front of the store in row after row of selections that ranged from classic wingtips to casual footwear to athletic shoes. And Tommy was the shoe department—had always been the shoe department for as long as anyone could remember. He kept index cards with each client's name, address, and phone number, as well as date of birth and the name(s) of their wives—past and present—and/or their girlfriends in alphabetical order in a locked metal box that sat next to the photograph of his grandparents' house on Crow Creek Road. On his desk too were a calculator, a phone, a pencil cup that held only sharpened No. 2 lead pencils, and one ink pen—a Mont Blanc—that, if he was completely honest, was used only to impress his clientele. And they were impressed—as much as with the gold Rolex he wore on his left wrist, even though the interest alone on the monthly payments would necessitate his continual payments for longer than he might be employed. But he was consumed with a seemingly untarnished image, assuming a role that would always be service-oriented rather than personally gratifying. And he seemed to fit that role without much effort, repeating the mundane cycle of what he knew his clients had come to expect.

Tommy had worked at Bailey & Sons since the day he graduated high school, settling into a daily routine with more and more comfort, more and more acceptance, even though I wondered if, like me, he was on a slow-burning coil inside that was getting warmer and warmer, the heat rising every day, until the day came when it would ignite everything in him that had been simmering for more years than he cared to recall. And suddenly, as if shaken from my imagined hallucinogenic stupor, I rush to the shoe stockroom to confirm that, in fact, there is something else that takes up space on Tommy's desk. I think it's a book.

I recall seeing a book on Tommy's desk, between the phone and the pencil holder, or was it sitting on the desk blotter that he recently added, the black desk blotter, with leather-like strips down the sides?

Yes, I'm certain, it was a book, but for the life of me I can't recall its title. And I find my anxiety rising, as if the book might disappear before I get there, like a sinister game of hide and seek. And there it is, *Newton's Laws of Motion*, an image of a launched rocket headed for the clouds on the cover. And I furrow my brows, wondering why Tommy would have a copy of *Newton's Laws of Motion*. And I'm pained trying to recall Newton's Laws, knowing though that there were three and knowing further that my lunch break will include a brief re-education of those laws on Google. Knowing that they had something—perhaps everything—to do with motion and force and resistance. And, once again, I am chilled from head to toe, even as the outside heat and humidity seem to make their way through every crevice, every entry, as I try with every ounce of energy to keep them out.

Eight

Tommy's car was already parked in the store lot when I pulled in off Washington Street, the morning traffic heavy with erratic drivers. I knew he would be waiting in the car, listening to the classic rock and roll radio station, checking his hair in the rearview mirror, acknowledging my arrival with the lift of his right hand as I pulled my car into the spot beside him, turning off the same radio station, and checking my recently-cropped jet black hair in the rearview mirror, noticing a few strands of gray beginning to surface, shoulders shrugged at the inevitable. It was a day that mimicked all other days at Bailey & Sons Outfitters.

One flowed into the next without any interference. It seemed as if we each exited and closed the door of our cars as if on cue. That wasn't the first time, either. As annoying as it was, we seemed to do so many of life's daily mundane motions at the exact same time in the exact same way: pulling into the parking lot, closing our car doors, reaching for the same door to enter the store, greeting clients, eating lunch, suffering through mid-afternoon boredom, and on and on, until we each once again opened the same car door, started our engines, and headed for a home that, for each of us, would be empty when we arrived. And it's the day-to-day certainty of structure that builds an intense momentum that isn't recognized until it crescendos and begins to unravel from its own mundane habits. And something told me that we each ate for dinner what was easiest to make—a cold ham sandwich or a bowl of cereal with a sprinkle of too-ripe berries—sitting in front of the television, watching programs that we weren't really watching, but feeling something even more numbing than loneliness.

We were mirror images of each other's unimpressive lives, and yet we maneuvered our daily activities as if nothing unusual was happening. And it was perhaps in those moments of recognition that we abhorred one another the most, knowing that the other knew exactly how we felt, exactly how frightened we were of the loneliness that was slowly and yet most certainly sweeping over us in a wave that was gathering the momentum of a tsunami.

"Good morning, Alex. You look really nice today. Love the outfit," Tommy said as he took one last, long drag from his cigarette, discarding the butt in the gun-metal receptacle. I wondered for just a split second what, in fact, I had chosen to wear to work today. The black leather ballet flats were most certainly chosen, as they were most mornings. And, my black linen ankle-length slacks could be worn only because I stood up all day long, walking around the store, assisting clients; otherwise, the "million-dollar" wrinkle that naturally accompanies linen garments would never have been acceptable at Bailey & Sons. And even though the heavy summer heat and humidity would already define the day's weather as it had throughout its yearly, repeated cycle, I chose a lightweight, salmon-colored, crewneck, cable cashmere sweater, and an Hermès scarf that belonged to my mother tied at the neck, knowing that the air conditioning inside the store would register steady at 68 degrees. Tied, the design of skiers on a snow-capped mountain, sprigs of holly berries sprinkled about like fairy dust was not discernible to anyone, not known to anyone but me.

As I caught myself in the shining, front double glass doors of the store, I was surprised at the minuscule size that stared back at me, as if I didn't recognize the image at all, and together we walked to the employee side entrance. "Good morning," I returned. "It's going to be another scorcher, isn't it? I think I may just wilt and die like a withering vine, before fall arrives," and Tommy held open the door for me to enter.

The days, weeks, months, holidays, and seasons moved with the certainty of the hands of a well-wound watch, never missing a beat, never gifting more than either of us expected. It was as if we were both stuck in place, with the rest of the world engaging in whatever the rest of the world engages in. Our options were limited and yet neither of us made the least bit of effort to turn back the hands of time, for they had already passed. Even the years ticked by with a taunting that was maddening. Some mornings—and this one was one of those mornings—I looked at Tommy and was attracted to his neatness, his seeming strong sense of self, his pride in representing a company he had worked with for the past 20 years, gathering an impressive list of clients who depended on him—regardless of the degree—to outfit them in their footwear, business or casual. And his dedication and commitment to achieving that end was something that was certainly to be admired. He took his job seriously. He knew his clients' full names and whether they preferred to be addressed by their first name or their surname. He knew which ones wanted a beverage, which ones needed assistance in trying on shoes, and which ones trusted him with their personal secrets: their mistresses, their health issues, and their emotional distresses.

And all of these, while perhaps making themselves known to others, were closely guarded by Tommy, and perhaps that is why the core of each indiscretion became Tommy's alone—a gatekeeper of sorts of others' secrets. And upon further reflection, maybe this was enough for Tommy, and he might have suspected the same of me.

Bailey & Sons operated like the cylinders of an ocean liner, in complete synchronicity. Staff reported to work Monday through Saturday, on time, with the spit and polish of an enlisted army battalion. And yet, they each kept tucked inside their back pockets secrets that while known by most were never openly discussed: verbal and emotional spousal abuse, divorces, extramarital affairs, prescription drug addictions.

The female staff was often victimized; their desperate need to be loved historically woven into the delicate fibers of the Appalachia they so fiercely found themselves a part of. And while generation after generation of these women knew their own strength and called on it with the regular precision of waking with the sounds of their morning alarm clocks, weathering the abuses of the men in their lives, just as steadfast were they in refusing to change the situation. And they went on, each one in their familiar everydayness of life's ups and downs, choosing to focus on the ups more than the downs by not ignoring them and sweeping them under the proverbial rug, but by acknowledging them for what they were: a part of life, a part of their life, a part that they chose to bundle and not set to fire, but bundle nevertheless and box and wrap and set with a pretty silk ribbon and bow on the back of the top shelf in a closet used only for such refuse, imagining the day—the one fine day—when, in fact, they just might be prompted to light the accumulation of bundles with one fierce match, the flames igniting their own abhorred inadequacies, as they each became nearly robotic in their daily schedules—a bit like sleepwalkers hoping not to fall off a very precarious edge.

And as much as I knew this—all of this—to be true for not only others but for myself as well, the nausea that overwhelmed me whenever I recognized its truth often found me walking briskly through the store to the ladies' room to relieve myself of the rancid taste that had built up within me like a delicate house of cards that one slow, even breath could destroy.

Tommy's weekly schedule included, without exception, Friday and Saturday evenings spent at the movie theater a few blocks east of Bailey & Sons. He preferred this smaller venue to the multiplex theater that was located in a congested retail area situated on a mountaintop located 15 minutes from downtown and because he enjoyed the short walk from the shop, leaving his car in the parking lot and walking the few blocks between the two points. And he always chose to walk on the store side of the street rather than on the opposite side, where a boarded building that had been a part of Charleston's west side for longer than anyone could recall had recently burned from an interior wiring malfunction. At least that was what had been reported. No one ever walked on that side of the street.

The graphic and disturbing graffiti that had grown over time to embellish what remained of the exterior was unsettling to even the most hard-edged. And no one wanted to walk past an establishment that for decades had been a known Mafia cover for illicit gambling, prostitution, and other ills that seemed to infiltrate even the finest of cities. And I had noticed a few days ago that someone had spray-painted words in Italian that no one was particularly interested in translating.

His propensity for movies ran to the bizarre, the dramatic, and particularly the unsolved crime mysteries, with crimes of passion and the macabre drawing him in like a poisonous elixir—drinking it all in, nonetheless, drop by drop. And I found this adhesion surprising. Not that I expected Tommy to be attracted to wholesome cinema only, but to discover that his attraction bordered on the edge as much as it did, caught me unaware and yet curious. *The Girl with the Dragon Tattoo* became so intoxicating for Tommy that he returned weekend after weekend to watch the film, stating on Monday morning that he had to keep returning (when most of us barely made it through one screening) in order to remember every burning detail of the dialogue and every minute detail of each scene's footage. And he was so deeply moved by Ryan Gosling's performance in *Drive* that he made a pair of brown, kid leather driving gloves part of his winter wardrobe, clenching the steering wheel in an eerie mimicry and then deciding to wear them every day. But I think it was *The Mechanic* that introduced him to a way of life that, until the screening, was just that—a movie screening. And while it didn't necessarily become real to Tommy, he wanted it to become real. And then, as if to do nothing but completely make his Monday morning recreations and critiques even more mysterious, he returned to *Midnight in Paris* with an unbridled loyalty, analyzing and analyzing again and again the meaning behind it all, knowing with complete conviction that the meaning was so very subjective—and yet, he would bring it up over and over and over, until one by one we each turned away, knowing that in his mind, Tommy would continue the conversation, albeit one-sided. And we knew, too, that he found nothing unusual about this behavior.

And while I mysteriously yearned to become a part of those conversations in a very detailed way, I imagined the conversations and played them out in my most private moments, afraid to let both Tommy and myself know of my yearnings for conversations that would most certainly be much too revealing—at least for myself. And once revealed, there would be no going back; the only direction being one fraught with a paradoxical danger. And while we never attended a movie together, I often waited to find out on Monday morning from Tommy what he had seen the previous weekend. After having read Larsson's novel, I couldn't have possibly attended the movie version with anyone but myself. And while there were moments throughout the reading of the novel that both enraged and titillated me, I kept that to myself. And it was one movie that when Tommy reported having seen it, he said very little about it and neither did I. And for that reticence, I was grateful. And yet it was for that very reason that I was also so acutely aware of scenes that for both of us were all too inviting, all too revealing, and that's when I was overcome with a fear that was fueled by an imagination that was anything but innocent, anything but pure.

And while those moments of regression frightened me, they also spoke to me throughout the day and into the evening in a whispered interlude—a taunting—as if hiding in my pocket or perched on my shoulder, a constant reminder of who I truly was in the depths of my soul, of who I had perhaps always been, of who I had tried so very hard—so very diligently—to ignore, as if by my very efforts it would magically somehow happen just because I wanted it to. And as I at times begged it too to desert me, I held on tight to its sick taunts, secretly wanting to know each delicate, destructive layer. And each time this cycle of heightened awareness began, I was polarized, thinking that perhaps Tommy had caught a glimpse of me at the same movie, while believing all along that I was a blip on a screen.

It was *The Descendants*, though, that both troubled me and held me in its grasp long after I walked a healthy distance from Tommy on a starless night, both of us entering the movie theater on our own and yet together. Whether Tommy ever knew that I was keeping my distance from him, I can't be sure. But I recall wanting to be in that movie theater with him, without being with him at all. And knowing that he would stop at the concession stand—because he believed that buttered popcorn, a Coca-Cola, and a box of peanut M&M's were essential to the occasion—I waited a bit at the corner of Washington and Laidley Streets before entering the theater and purchasing my ticket, sans stopping at the concession stand, knowing that he had already entered the dark theater.

I walked into the theater and took a seat on the end of the last row on the right side, a wall shielding me from others. Tommy was seated at the end of a row at the center of the theater on the left side, where when he crossed his left leg and rested his ankle on his right knee, there was room in the aisle to accommodate his polished cordovan loafer, which seemed to take on a ghostly glow that captivated me throughout the movie, glistening sporadically as it met light from the screen, like a firefly coming and going, which I found more than a bit alluring. And occasionally, he would run his slender fingers through his hair, and I found myself desperately wanting to be the one to do it for him, while shaking the thought from my reverie.

As the lights dimmed, a young couple who were more engaged in groping one another than they were in either their concessions or what was on the screen, sat a few rows in front of me. I tried very hard to look the other way, knowing that I could not have what they so eagerly gave to one another. And as the film played, I cried not knowing whether it was for the characters and the roles they played or for my own inability to acknowledge what was happening in my own life, what would happen if the loneliness several rows in front of me would do with the loneliness that occupied my own seat in a dark movie theater that housed more secrets than anyone knew, and I trembled at the thought.

And when I first saw the trembling of Tommy's shoulders, I was deeply moved at his aloneness, knowing that it matched my own; and because the heartache was too deeply felt, I exited the theater, going out into the darkened night, the moon a slender sliver of light, headed home to a space filled with more loneliness and heartache.

Nine

As the years moved along in an almost meaningless way and holidays seemed to come in and out of focus, Tommy and I arrived and departed every workday (for I had made the decision to work full-time in order to maintain some sort of normalcy in an otherwise abnormal life) as if our very clocks were set by our own comings and goings, as if the clocks dominated—an incessant tick-tock, tick-tock.

"Structure," Tommy announced one early spring morning, "is a good thing, right?"

"I suppose," I answered, shaking the light rain from my yellow rain jacket, and setting my opened umbrella inside the employee entrance in a corner reserved for just that purpose.

"I mean, I read an article just the other day—I can't recall where—that spoke to that very thing. Structure, routine, is essential to our well-being. It gives us a reason to get up in the morning, a purpose."

"Hmm. And all along I thought the reason to get up every morning was simply to do exactly what I did every morning: wake, take my vitamins, shower, brush my teeth, dress, and grab a dry bagel as I headed out the door for work, knowing with complete certainty that I'd meet some jerk along the way who was either driving and trying without much success to apply mascara, or switching lanes without any notice whatsoever, or God forbid texting a message that I'm certain had relatively little importance. But now you're telling me that there's some redeeming quality to all this daily monotony, this completely uninteresting, tedious repetition of the same routine day in and day out?"

"That's exactly what I'm trying to tell you, Alex. That in the tedious repetition, as you call it, there is purpose. The article went on to say that there is actually joy in the mundane. That it sets us up for not only the expected, but that if we look closely, it will reveal the unexpected. And it is in the unexpected where we find our purpose." And with that revelation, Tommy finished off his first cup of coffee.

"Well, I'm not sure if I want to get that reflective, that analytical about the whole thing. I mean, we each get up every morning and do exactly what is expected of us. Nobody is surprised, unless of course there is news of devastation or political upheaval or, bringing it closer to home, the filing of a divorce or the death of a family member. I mean, generally speaking, the day just becomes the day. And moments of joy are not necessarily expected or anticipated. And surprise is hidden from us, or else it wouldn't be a surprise."

"I agree, but I also think that when those moments of surprise materialize, we find ourselves either embracing them or running as fast as we can from them. I like to think our purpose is not in the daily, mundane rituals, but in what might come from those moments—what might propel us to change direction. And I think it's in those moments that the very surprise that waits is met with a mix of fevered excitement and heightened awareness; and even though we might find it disturbing, we move towards it anyway, unable to do much else."

And as I checked myself in the full-length mirror, applying my smile as broadly as I could without seeming to be too harried by the accompanying pretensions, I wondered not only at who was looking back, but at Tommy's profile, set in a rigid determination, a near-robotic stance over which he had little control. And I froze, wondering how close I might be to the truth. I have recalled this mysterious and unsettling conversation so frequently that it, too, has become a part of my daily routine, even as I try to close my eyes and shake my head, as if to awaken from a deep stupor, still unsuccessful at every attempt.

As spring moved into summer at an agonizingly slow pace, much like the hour of sadness that follows a death, the heat and humidity rising proportionately, I recalled the slow-moving scene from the movie *The Untouchables* where the stairway shootout is filmed in slow motion; Kevin Costner's character takes out the bad guys, while Andy García's character saves the day with the toss of a handgun, sliding as if into home plate, stopping the baby carriage with the lift of his right leg, while the baby remains blissfully oblivious. And I am envious at each one's ability to control what appears to be out of control.

And as the expected heat and humidity arrived and settled across the valley, I noticed too that Tommy seemed to carry with him a level of anxiety that I had not seen before, which, over time, became a cumbersome albatross, a burden to be carried as a penance for what I had not yet discovered. Even his posture seemed to reflect this new, unwelcomed companion, as little by little over the course of the summer his shoulders became more and more rounded, his head bending lower and lower until, as if recognizing the changes himself, he straightened both and returned to his former self.

"Tommy," I ventured one particularly slow, late Friday afternoon, "are you okay? Is something bothering you? I don't mean to pry, but you just seem a bit out of sorts lately." I knew that I was breaking my own rules of engagement with Tommy, who I always kept at bay for nothing more than pure instinct, but I watched him drift in and out of his normally confident persona to one of a near-catatonic state, his hands slightly trembling and his hair growing longer than usual. Too, he engaged less and less in idle conversation with his clients who, while not seeming to notice, often walked out of the store with a quizzical look on their face.

"Just thinking about a lot," Tommy replied. "Mostly things that I can't do much about," he continued. And then, I made the mistake of asking, "What things?" And I knew before I spoke the last word that I shouldn't have spoken either of them. I knew that was the turning point, but it was too late. I had spoken them, and things would never again be as they had been. What I should have said was, "Sorry. I hope things work out," or something to that effect. But opening the door for the conversation to continue would turn out to be a mistake—a mistake from which I could never recover, for it brought forth an enumeration that revealed more than I cared to know, one that would even bring with it an unfamiliar trepidation that would haunt me for months to come.

"Oh, you know, things that affect our lives without our having much power to do anything about." I stood there, listening to the beginnings of Tommy's ruminations, hoping that there would be a deluge of customers into the store, but also recognizing the unlikelihood of that actually happening, as the certainty of the heavy weight of a summer rain arrived in sheets, blowing the store's awnings in the fierce winds, the sounds of heavy raindrops ricocheting off the store's thick, glass windows. The air conditioning seemed colder than usual, and I took from my shoulders the black cardigan that I had draped earlier and slid each arm into the sleeves. But it was my bare feet tucked snug inside my ballet flats that felt the chill most, and I looked at my watch to discover that there was yet a full hour before I could get home to the safety of my surroundings and pull on some heavy socks to warm my feet, or at the very least tuck them underneath as I sought refuge in the familiar folds of my well-worn chair.

"Do you think you have power over everything, Alex?"

"Not everything, no."

"Okay, let's play a game."

"I'd rather not, Tommy."

"Oh, come on, be a sport. Play, if for no other reason, than to simply humor a co-worker." I let escape a chuckle that I had thought I'd kept to myself, but it came out nevertheless, and I could see that it gave Tommy just what he had wanted: more than a bit of confidence. "Name five things in your life that you have absolutely no power over—no control."

I looked around the store to discover that most of the staff was gathered at the front and back windows, watching the storm build, checking their own watches and probably wishing they, like me, could leave and go home to a more subdued space, one where they could kick off their shoes and seek shelter in a favored spot, in favored clothes, and in a favored, real self—a self that wasn't on, one that was in hibernation, until the alarm sounded the following morning and they began the often arduous regimen of the day.

"Hmm, five things over which I have no power or control. Well, actually, control and power are often two very different things, wouldn't you agree?" And without much persuasion at all from Tommy, I found myself more easily than I'd like to admit engaging in a conversation that I knew would lead me in a direction that I didn't want to go, and I was both irritated with myself and eerily charmed by Tommy's ability to draw me into the conversation, like a hypnotist. And without my consciously knowing it, I hoped the conversation would bring intrigue. And I was puzzled at the dichotomy that was becoming obvious. It was more than strangely paradoxical and more than strangely disturbing, and yet I moved forward with it, wondering at the unexpected.

"How so?"

"Well," I began, "power generally refers to someone's ability to influence what another person does; while control seems, I don't know, a bit more aggressive."

"But if someone has power over you, doesn't that mean that you lose all control over yourself?"

"Makes sense, and yet I think there is a definite difference between the two."

"Let's make it easy then. You pick which one you want to talk about and we'll start there."

"Oh, Tommy, I..." The lightning and thunder picked up in intensity, and I jumped at both the streak of glaring light and the roaring sounds from an angry thunder, as if both were new phenomena which I had never before experienced—as if each were acting as reminders to guard closely what I was about to say. And yet somehow, I was ignoring what was tapping with such ferocity on my shoulder. And with the store void of customers and staff gathered at the windows, emitting exclamations of wonder and worry that seemed to echo throughout the lifeless shelves and racks of fashions meant to ornament the human body, we both began to laugh uproariously, thinking of the absurdity of the moment.

"Oh, come on, Alex, it's just a game. I mean since there's nobody in the store, and the storm is kicking up a mighty force, and everyone else is, for some reason, entranced by its power, why don't you give it a try. It's not a big deal, but it is a bit more interesting than joining the forces at the windows. Hmm, I believe I just used the word power. So, if it will help, I'll go first. I have no power or control over the storm that is making itself known with such aggression. There, how's that for a conversation starter?"

"Oh, alright. Truthfully, neither of us has any control or power over the storm that is gathering outside the walls of this well-respected establishment. However, I believe the original question was more personal. You had asked me to name five things over which I have no control or power over, correct?"

"Correct," Tommy said with an unpleasant playfulness and a determined nod of his head and a tone that suggested there was no turning back, and I relinquished all my innate power and control to something much more certain than anything I had been or could ever be. I noticed that with that response, Tommy wore a slight grin that carried with it more than a hint of a flirtatious undertone, and I felt both an attraction and a revulsion building inside me—an attraction because I couldn't deny the allure of the slight grin and revulsion because it seemed to me that Tommy's usually squeaky-clean hair was a bit disheveled, with specks of dandruff scattered on the shoulders of his navy sport coat that I had never before noticed. And his generally high-polished shoes appeared to have more than a few scuff marks on the tops.

I closed my eyes and gave my head a light shake, reopening them, hoping that my sudden discoveries had been a mirage. And yet, they hadn't been. And it was then that I began to want to delve further into Tommy's hidden inadequacies, as if it was the only thing in the world that mattered. And then, as if in complete union with the growing storm, I began to realize that he might not only be everything I had thought him to be, but that his clever manipulation had begun to surface above the storm, laying everything else at his feet. And I dismissed this troubling awareness in order to play a game that I instinctively knew was fraught with danger.

We both stood facing each other, and Tommy reached over with his right hand, using his index finger to move a short strand of hair that had fallen in front of my left eye to its rightful place behind my ear, stopping briefly at the center of the back of my ear, before his finger slid down, gracing the back of the post of my pearl stud earring, and I was as aroused as if we had just made passionate love on a snowy, Sunday afternoon before a lightly-crackling fire, the glow from the embers the only light. And we both stood there as if holding our breaths, as the lightning and thunder continued its potentially destructive interlude, each of us locking eyes, my lips opened just enough to invite whatever he wanted to give. And I knew, as certainly that the storm would eventually pass, that we had closed the chasm that had kept us comfortable for longer than perhaps either of us had wanted.

I was filled with a trepidation that as incredulous as it may seem, was as powerful as it was unfamiliar. I began to tremble, and Tommy didn't even attempt to hide his own vulnerabilities. And I think it was at that moment that I knew that what had been set in motion was unlikely to reverse a direction that, while both of us wanted to run from, we instead ran right to, tossing any hesitation as if it were a weightless feather that simply wouldn't move along its trained trajectory, instead floating mindlessly from one powerful gust of wind to another, as in a game of harmless catch on the schoolhouse yard, children at recess.

"Alex?"

"Tommy?"

"Alex, I know what you're thinking..."

"Please, Tommy. I know that what's about to happen is going to happen as if neither of us has any power over it whatsoever. I think you know this, too. It's about setting in motion what has been determined beforehand, isn't it? And the more we try to force ourselves to resist what is certain, we actually relinquish all power and simply go where it had planned to take us all along."

"Alex?"

And as the storm appeared to weaken, I exhaled deeply and relinquished all I could, all I had, to what had been waiting patiently in a very dark corner of my mind, my heart longing for even the most miniscule amount of attention.

Ten

As fall approached and the autumnal colors of the Appalachian Mountains came into their fullness, Tommy and I took delicate and certain steps toward one another, brushing lightly against each other as we passed throughout the store, sharing a newfound appreciation for Oscar Mayer Lunchables, exchanging cheddar for American and chocolate chip cookies for vanilla cream.

Each exchange was the epitome of simplemindedness, but the slight touch of fingers to fingers during each exchange was what led to each succeeding one. And we each looked forward to the next with the anticipation that grew only from an earlier teenage game of spin-the-bottle at a birthday party. It was tantalizing in a way that was so very familiar and yet so very forbidden; but we played anyway. And as I from time to time intentionally let fall another strand of hair into my sight line, Tommy never missed the opportunity to travel the sensual path from my forehead to the side of my face, gently sending the lone strand back behind my ear. And when I began to welcome these seemingly innocent dalliances with the slow-moving close of my eyelids, inhaling and exhaling as if from a heightened awareness, Tommy began to respond by moving the tip of his slightly chapped index finger along the length of my arm, from my shoulder to my fingers, eventually locking those appendages, neither of us hesitating, but instead surrendering to all that we kept locked inside, knowing that trying to keep it arrested was no longer an option.

"Alex, would you please help Tommy bring down from the attic the boxes of Christmas decorations?" Betty Williams, the long-time store manager asked, as she continued to stamp the pile of Christmas cards that Bailey & Sons mailed to all its clients, making certain not to ever send a card with a greeting that read *Merry Christmas* to the countless number of Jewish patrons, which far outnumbered the Christians. And the engraved company signature under the *Happy Holidays* inside greeting matched the indigo blue on everything that read Bailey & Sons Outfitters. And every Bailey from the beginning to the current owners took tremendous pride in the uniqueness that identified them alone.

I took the elevator to the top floor, which was considered the attic, and met Tommy, who had changed out of his starched white Oxford button-down to a worn flannel shirt that was more handsome than anything I had ever seen him wear. And he, too, seemed more comfortable in its private history than I had ever been in my own skin. And I found myself wanting to know its stories: what it had seen, what it had felt, what it had heard, what it knew, for I suddenly felt that it—this seeming simple object—knew everything there was to know about Tommy. And in continuing to look at it, it appeared to snicker at my ignorance—an ignorance that I was determined to reverse.

"Hi there," I said as Tommy's taut stomach was revealed as he lifted from a high shelf a box marked simply CHRISTMAS DECO-RATIONS. I walked over to where he balanced himself on the steplad-der and reached for the box.

"It's a bit heavy, Alex. I've got it."

I backed away just enough for Tommy to descend the small ladder. He bent at the waist, setting the box on the worn, hardwood floor, and I made certain to move just a few inches closer to him so that when he turned, he couldn't help but kiss me lightly on the mouth—a mouth that was waiting and so very eager to meet his. And as he turned toward me, he placed his arms around my waist and drew me to him, not as gently as I had imagined, but with a slight force that only left me wanting for more.

As much as I appeared to others a fragile China doll, I had more than a few cracks in my fine porcelain, and Tommy instinctively knew this about me, and I was grateful that the foreplay wasn't necessary. I was ravenous with desire—we both were—and as I touched the thin fibers of his flannel shirt, I pulled away from him and looked at the fraying collar and began to unbutton the front buttons of the shirt, as he stood still and let me. And neither of us stopped the other from doing what we had for so very long resisted, until those first hurried moments turned into hurried enrapture that define every intimate encounter that is resisted for much longer than necessary, until the growing climax ruptures and what ensues is an appetite for more—always for more. And as we lay together among a box long upturned of strings of multi-colored lights and shiny orbs of ornaments and one gleaming, five-point star, the old tin copper ceiling seemed to pick up our reflection, and nothing and yet everything seemed more pronounced than ever before.

And for one brief moment, we thought of nothing else but the next time, knowing that it would return again and again, until our appetites had been satiated or needed something even more daring than we could have ever anticipated.

Several months before Tommy and I were to drive to his grandparents' house, I began to find a reason to leave just shortly after Tommy left the store in order to follow him to his house, about a 15-minute drive east of the store. And while Tommy, as was the case with the rest of the store personnel, kept mostly to himself and at times was both reticent and at others completely transparent, I was most attracted to the former, wanting desperately to meld it to the latter. I had discovered from his Uncle Mike one day when I lunched alone that Tommy's parents had been ordered to release Tommy to the custody of his paternal grandparents when he was just a toddler.

His parents had been cruel to him, first one then the other subjecting him to beatings; once he was left unconscious after his father threw him down the basement stairs, landing on a pile of old quilts and discarded rugs. The neighbors heard Tommy's screams and called the police as Tommy's father fled the house. Once the police arrived, one of the officers picked up Tommy from the bottom of the basement stairs and rushed him to the hospital, where staff called the officials and had Tommy given over to the courts. Within 24 hours, his parents were arrested and his grandparents gained custody of young Tommy.

"He's had a rough life, Alex. He never recovered—not really—from the abuse his parents inflicted on him. Maybe nobody does. I mean, how could anyone survive it? Oh, he lets on that he's fine, but don't we all?"

And I realized that maybe my earlier assessment of Uncle Mike had been wrong, and I was filled with compassion for them both, knowing now why Uncle Mike tried so very hard to make Tommy feel special. And it was with this knowledge that my need to know as much about him as I could gain grew in a most ferocious manner. Yes, we were both loners, but loners whose hearts had been trampled in ways that were completely out of our control, out of our power. It rested with those with whom we had entrusted that power and control. And it occurred to me what a shame it is that we don't possess this knowledge from the beginning, but rather as the end approaches, and the familiar chills that had somehow become a very real part of my very soul gathered into a frightening cloud that walked every step with me, as if over shattered and glistening shards of glass.

The first time I saw Tommy pull his shiny black Corvette onto the pea-gravel driveway of an unincorporated coal mining town east of Charleston, I was certain that he must be pulling into a property that belonged to someone else. It was a much smaller version of his grandparents' house farther east, but in so many ways similar in its collapsing state.

It was a white clapboard-sided house in much need of a power-washing. Its single front window was cracked at one pane, and another pane had been boarded up. *No,* I thought, *this can't be Tommy's house.* There were no steps at the front of the house, so that when Tommy entered, he had to jump from the barren patch of front yard to the rotting, wooden-slated front porch. There was no storm door, and the front door was coated with a light black soot of coal ash that I suspected had always been there, building layer upon layer of the fine dust. Two unfinished wooden columns held up the overhanging asphalt roof. There was a single, metal folding chair with a ripped fabric seat on the front porch beside the door, a malnourished, possible feral cat discouraging any visitors.

I had parked my car farther up a bit and across the road from the house, but still within full view. The only hint of color or pattern came from a faded floral sheet that hung haphazardly at the front window. Alongside the far side of the house was an overgrown clematis, whose leaves looked as if they hadn't had a drink of water for longer than they could remember. Even with the recent rains, the drops seemed as if to pass by knowing that any attempt at nourishment would be wasted on something that had long ago expired.

The front yard was barren of anything green and vibrant, instead overrun with rocks strewn here and there and noticeable dips that would challenge not only the scrawny, mixed-breed, malnourished beagle that seemed to be in search of even a slight morsel of anything edible, but Tommy, who seemed with clear memory to know where to avoid stepping, as if crossing a mine field. The rusted, chain link, partial fence that marked the property borders was next to a chemical plant that emitted vaporous clouds of noxious fumes that permeated the area in near-isolation, triangular-shaped yellow biohazard danger signs in clear view. And yet, children played, and residents came and went, and the childlike, melodious tunes from an ice-cream truck attempted to negate the obvious.

Tommy entered through the front door, scraping his loafers on the thin brown mat, and closed the door, as a single exposed outside bulb flickered. I drove in a near trance to the alley at the back of the house to discover a completely different landscape, as if I had just awakened from a dream and found myself walking down the yellow brick road. It was pristine. Everything about it was pristine. My first thought as I tried to work my way through the beauty that was looking back at me was that it looked so very much like the cover of the latest issue of *Southern Living*: a garden in full bloom—both flower and veg-etable, with a small patch of succulent rhubarb, its luster of healthy, pink stalks ripe and begging to be diced into firm pieces for a summer pie. And I closed my eyes to envision a curl of steam escaping from thin slits in a buttery crust. And the sweet taste of the sugary vegetable became real, as I closed my eyes and licked my lips.

The rose bushes were meticulously tended, and the brilliant hues of the hibiscus, the deep purple of the amaranth, and the soft greens from the sea holly, blinding in their brightness. But it was the tower-ing sunflowers among the low-lying marigolds that pleaded for atten-tion that brought me to exit my car and walk through the healthy foliage, stopping to gaze from the seat of a grass-green, high-gloss painted Adirondack chair without reminding myself that Tommy was just steps away. A black, metal sign was attached to the chair's back with a quote by Eleanor Roosevelt that I recalled learning from my mother. I don't recall ever sharing it with Tommy. *I once had a rose named after me and I was very flattered. But I was not pleased to read the description in the catalogue: No good in a bed, but fine up against a wall.*

In the past, those words had made me laugh uncontrollably; but now, the tears fell in abundance without my knowing why. A highly detailed antique wrought-iron fence set the garden off from everything else around it, and its charm became an elixir on which I yearned to become blissfully inebriated. A yellow and white striped canvas covering kept the strong rays of the sun at bay, and as I soaked up all the beauty it graciously gave away, I saw Tommy standing at the only window at the back of the house: a brand new Pella wood-cased window that he cranked open from which to wave a hand that seemed as fragile as the blossoms on the rose petals, and I tried to catch the tears that fell, not knowing for whom they were intended.

Eleven

The evening we left for Tommy's grandparents' house was unseasonably cool.

Driving along Route 16 South, the Volvo's sunroof open, the light breeze picked up strands of our hair, sending them on a journey all their own through the heavy forest, the gentle lapping of the waters below the bridge, and I felt as if everything I had ever been or done in my life had led up to this point of surrender to what would never be, could never be. And I closed my eyes and placed my hand on his inner right thigh, the feel of his charcoal gray worsted wool trousers smooth against my touch. He didn't turn to look at me; instead, his gaze on the winding road, the canopy of trees hovering over us, appeared transparent as glass. My chocolate-brown linen slacks billowed, and the wind found an entry at the top, unbuttoned opening of my baby blue Pima cotton tailored shirt.

I felt a chill and was glad that I had remembered to grab my brown cashmere cardigan, with an orange thread woven throughout. My feet, though, were chilled as they nestled inside my scalloped, navy Chloé ballet flats. I even felt the chill of the air as it lit upon my pearl studs. And yet, there was a stream of warmth that seemed to flow through my veins, and I was comforted in a way that I'd not been for a very long time, knowing that the unrelenting, slow-moving pain that had attached itself to me as a leech would soon be over. Tommy wore his polished cordovan loafers without any socks and, looking down at his feet, I wanted nothing more than to touch the softness of his skin—to feel it against my own. The cuffs of his white Oxford button-down shirt were turned inside the sleeve, his Rolex glistening in the early evening light, the tip of his Mont Blanc peeking out from his front pocket, his gaze never leaving the road. I moved my left hand to carry his rich locks away from his eyes, but even that movement didn't appear to alter his gaze; his concentration was on arriving where we both were so urgent to be, to begin a journey that held so very many secrets that we were so eager to reveal, if to no one else other than ourselves; for it was our own self-imposed incarceration that had held us prisoner for longer than we even knew; a conditioning from which we'd never emerge victorious.

And as I closed my eyes to the certain relinquishment of self, Frank Sinatra's "Fly Me to the Moon" played, soft and sweet and inviting, as our destination became clear in the sliver of moonlight, as it played hopscotch along the surface of the creek's crystal, clear waters.

Tommy signaled our right-hand turn onto Crow Creek Road, the Volvo sending up pieces of gravel intermittently along the way to his grandparents' house, occasionally ricocheting off the car, Tommy and I both appearing oblivious to the sounds and the potential damage. We pulled off the gravel road onto the overgrown yard. There was no garage or carport, just a rusty old Ford pickup truck to greet us, its blue paint faded and chipped in so many places that it resembled a rough checkerboard pattern. An overgrowth of fungi and weeds called the back cab home. There were no tires left on the truck, as it sat with an unusual formality on top of cracked cinderblock.

The stench was overwhelming, the windows completely gone, and the flies swarming all around as if certain to uncover something on which to feed. And yet, as I exited the Volvo, the warm breeze invited outstretched arms that mimicked the swaying tree branches, and I felt as if I could fly. A primitive piece of tree bark dangled from a single hook at the side porch, "Gone Fishin'" crudely written in saffron paint. On another rusted hook was a fraying, camouflaged fishing vest with dried worms clinging to the front pockets. There was a broken-legged wooden beach chair with a soiled, faded striped canvas covering. Crude sapling fishing poles were wedded in the soggy ground, their lines moving slightly, as evening set in. A metal bucket with faint lettering that had at one time read "Bait" was holding on to the last bits of algae-infested rainwater, and beside it, a straw fishing sack, rife with holes that could have only been created by river rats.

Closer to the creek were a petrified canoe and a broken oar. And alongside it, a long-extinguished campfire, remnants of charred twigs and shriveled marshmallows, a swarm of bees circling for possibilities. And resting on the edge of the sloped yard nearby was a mildewed red and green plaid sleeping bag, an overweight river rat crawling out from the inside flap. And yet, I wasn't alarmed at much of anything about the decay and debris that surrounded me, for we were inching our way closer to adding to it.

My gaze journeyed to the part of the house that I imagined was the attic. And while I had read about them, I had never seen one until this moment. I accepted that what was about to happen was perhaps a part of something much more complex than I could ever possibly understand. Maybe what had caught my eye was a part of something not only mysterious, but a bit magical. The witch window was the only window whose glass panes had not been shattered. And while I was feeling more than a bit apprehensive, it was matched by a feeling of complete and most-welcomed resignation. I furrowed my brow, wondering how an architectural feature that is found primarily in

Vermont farmhouses had made its way to the remote region of Appalachia. And as simple as their history, what was unfolding in front of me was not something that I would ever be able to completely understand. And for reasons unknown to me, I wasn't remotely interested in uncovering a single one of them.

"It wasn't always like this, Alex," Tommy's near-whispered voice disrupted my unhurried and unexplained calm, planting myself firmly back on familiar ground.

"I know," I said as I took his hand, and together we reached for the handle of the screen door that was held on by one hinge, opened the front door of the house, and entered the dilapidated dwelling, knocking down one cobweb after another, watching cockroaches and spiders and rodents scurry across the rotted cork floor, both of us still surprisingly so undaunted by the house's interior surroundings. And as I looked to a small entry table that had been hewn from white birch, I was mesmerized by a collection of a common loon feather, a dried sprig of black huckleberry, a petrified red russula, a loblolly pinecone, and a great spangled fritillary. The composite was nearly indescribable, a majestic setting for what was to come; a still life on an imagined canvas.

There were only four rooms in the small house. The living room had a crumbling brick fireplace and a crude wooden mantel that held a lineup of old rough plaster and ceramic candleholders, a few with the wax burned to a nub, streams of its rough residue clinging to the sides. There was faded, peeling wallpaper on the wall that, once cleaned, would reveal its once-visible pattern of poppies and daffodils. In the kitchen, a single, flat panel curtain hung at the window, nailed at each corner. It too was once vibrant with its curling stream of yellow daises and a border of red dashes and solid lines, as if in a Morse code message. The kitchen wallpaper was hanging by a slender thread, its barbed-wire pattern much too revealing. On the windowsill sat a lineup of old glass bottles in all shades of green and red and light blue. I imagined them washed and dried, the sun glistening through each.

I heard the flush of a toilet and turned to see Tommy standing on a sunken, leaf-strewn, linoleum floor, an opened window blowing in more leaves and debris from outside, the cracked porcelain sink rusted at the drain. He looked at me with a mysterious but settled gaze, and I looked back at him, both of us knowing that the time was drawing near, both of us walking towards it and each other with complete conviction, void of doubt, certain of a plan we had rehearsed so many times that it had become a scene from a movie we had seen over and over and over again.

"There's something I want you to do first, before we move forward with our plan," he managed to say with a familiar ease.

"I know," I replied. "I've always known this would happen first. I've been anticipating it for much too long, and I think you have, too."

"Yes," he said, discovering his voice to be just a tad bit mechanized.

"Are you sure?" I asked.

"Yes," he replied, with a tone not unlike that of an automaton. And as Tommy reached for my hand, we walked together into the only bedroom in the house, into a past that had not, miraculously and most incredulously, been disturbed, as if it had instead been preserved. And I was mesmerized by the four-poster iron bed dressed in pure white sheeting, a rich monogram—T&A—heavily embroidered in a dense, deep crimson. And on a wall shelf were stacked bolt after bolt of Pima cottons in European prints: a burgundy background with scattered Jack Russells, a pink floral, a pastel plaid, a field of grass with tiny slithering snakes, a bold Hawaiian print, a rich paisley, and a tiny, pink rosebud on a black background. The newly installed rich brown hardwood floor glowed, picking up the light from the flame of a single candle, whose scent of jasmine wafted throughout the room.

I breathed in its elixir and opened my arms to welcome Tommy, while the eerie yet inviting sounds from the cracked porcelain face of a doll propped on a rocking chair in the corner of the room began to speak: "Come play with me. No one is watching." And then the voice taunted with a sinister giggle, ending with, "Please don't drop me again. I don't like that. It hurts," as a tinkling of piano keys sounded in the background—an indisputable dichotomy between the building thunderstorm and the sweeping of the tree limbs against the decaying, clapboard house and the rising waters of the crystal clear creek.

And in the moments of the aftermath of one rapturous moment after another, what I most treasured was not its wild abandon but its childlike innocence, complete with the resolve that comes from the slow trickle of bittersweet tears.

After I showered and changed into a pair of Levi's and a fresh shirt, I walked out the same door of the house on Crow Creek Road I had entered not that long ago, knowing that every line of the script had been delivered with the exactitude that had been rehearsed again and again, leaving no stone left unturned. And when it was over, I took from the nightstand the small plastic bottle of holy water, the gold encrusted cross emblazoned on the front smooth against my skin and sprinkled the christened bed linens with drops of what I hoped would be laden with forgiveness and rebirth. And there was something so comforting about that accomplishment that I knew would offer the respite needed for the hour-long drive west, back to where it had all started.

As I walked away, I turned one last time to look around a room where we had both perhaps felt more at home than any space we had ever before inhabited. The reasons were irrelevant. The feeling was all that mattered. And as the candle burned down, the flicker of its flame was reflected in the sterling sheen on the knife that rested, cleaned, on the nightstand. As I started the Volvo's engine, the sound mingled with the sounds of a night that had been stilled, the chorus of cicadas providing a harmonic melody. The light warm breeze seemed to envelope me, offering a cushion from the inevitable chill.

As I headed home, I made mild adjustments to the brown, kid leather driving gloves and gripped the wheel. The Volvo hugged tight the curves along Route 16, and as I resisted the pull of the wheel to head into the deep ravine below, I was forced—beyond all power and control—to remain in motion, growing more gleeful at having been able to give someone what they couldn't give to themselves. The repeated and hauntingly beautiful sounds of "Letting Go" by Hennie Bekker made the journey all the more certain. Dutifully, I did what had been asked of me.

"I did it!" I shouted to the night sky. I had recited and followed every detail of the list of instructions over and over, until they became a mantra—a prayer that would release each of us from the demons that controlled us without any power from ourselves to control them. I was a willing student to a teacher that I had loved in ways I shouldn't have.

Twelve

Turning off the Volvo's lights as I approached The Harboring and pulling into the parking space, I searched for the key to unlock the front door. I had always, for reasons unknown even to me, kept my house key and my car key on separate rings. I had remembered that I had put the key to The Harboring in the pocket of my jeans and reached in to retrieve it. I looked to the dark, empty playground, lit only by the dim bulb from the back door's entrance.

I stood there for a brief moment, closed my eyes, and recalled the sounds from my childhood of children laughing, playing, and learning how to bargain one with the other. As I walked to the front door and inserted the key, the heat and humidity of that late summer season had managed to expand the doorframe just enough, until I had to wrest all my weight against its thickness in order to open its frame wide.

I stepped inside the entryway, hung the apartment key and the car key on one of the hooks on the board attached to the wall, and began the climb to the second level. I stopped midway to see the magnolia tree outside the window, but the darkened night had blocked it from my view. I climbed the remaining stairs, stopping to use the bathroom, looking around at the neatly arranged bars of soap and bottles of shampoo; the fragrance of lavender, all-too familiar, and the obsession with order suddenly revolting.

The hallucinations, the voices, began almost immediately. Time became specks of sand in an hourglass that dropped with excruciating precision. It wasn't just the voices and the visions that crept into my daily life, as much as the maddening consistency of it all, as if the inexorable journey had no end.

I often sought unexplainable solace in replaying that night at Crow Creek Road, but the growing paranoia caused me to often look over my shoulders, certain to find whatever I thought was lurking in the shadows, tapping me gently, running away like a child at play, the ghosts peeking out at me from eyes which only they could see. Sometimes, I would hide in a corner of the living room in a fetal position, praying for protection from a God I felt was no longer there. I kept the shades drawn at all times, and even the sounds that used to comfort me now toyed with me, and I clasped my hands over my ears to drown out the innocence that was no longer mine.

The evening Tommy's voice came to me frightened me in a way that was as unfamiliar as anything I had ever before experienced. "Alex," he said in a soft whisper, "come here."

"Alex, come here," he repeated, in an even fainter whisper.

"Go away. Please go away," I pleaded.

"Alex, come here," he said, and this time I could barely make out the words.

I sat huddled like a small child, pressed against the wall, as Tommy moved towards me. I was suddenly overcome with not only a fear that had grown to ensnare all of me but one to which I was nearly relinquishing all of myself to, and I felt the first drop of blood make its journey down my bare leg, as the serrated knife I held had grazed my wrist ever so gently, but enough to let me know that I had forgotten what I held. And as easily as he approached, he just as easily evaporated.

On Monday of the week that followed our time at Crow Creek Road, I called Bailey & Sons and let them know that I was not well and that I would need a few days to recover from what I could not identify.

"Oh, my dear," Betty Williams said with a deep concern that I suddenly embraced with a warmth I didn't know I still possessed.

"I'll be fine, I'm sure," I replied, and thanked her for her concern.

"Certainly, my dear. Do take care of yourself."

"Yes. Yes, I will," and I ended the call.

With the arrival of each succeeding morning that week, I rang Bailey & Sons once again, letting Betty know that my afflictions had not waned. Once again, she offered her good wishes for a speedy recovery, but not until she seemingly and matter-of-factly asked a question which I had not anticipated.

"Incidentally, Alex, have you heard from Tommy this week?"

"No, I haven't," I replied, grateful for the simplicity of my words.

"I only ask because he has not been to the store this week, either. His car, though, is parked in his parking spot in the lot, but nobody has seen or heard from him since last Friday. We're all getting a bit concerned. We've tried to call him, but all calls are going to his voicemail."

"Oh my, I do hope nothing is wrong. Please let me know if you find out anything."

"Yes, of course, dear. And please get well soon, Alex. We miss you."

"Thank you, Betty," and I ended the call and wept like a child.

On Friday morning, I woke from a restless sleep, wearing the same clothes that I had worn since last Friday evening, putting on a baseball cap and dark sunglasses, as if that was all that was needed to disguise myself, to continue my childhood game of playing hooky, hoping I didn't run into classmates or teachers who would wonder at my week-long absence and my sudden recovery.

I arrived at Crow Creek Road just as the bulldozer had made its way down the gravel road that led to Tommy's grandparents' house. Collins Construction & Demolition had already arrived at the crumbling edifice on Crow Creek Road. The sun was bright, and the day was new. As the bulldozer started, it crept ever so slowly towards the house, and with very little effort it began to crumble and everything inside it folded into its own, as glass broke and fabric unraveled, and the faint cries from an old doll whose voice spoke only to me echoed throughout the mountain laurel, carried off by the gentle lapping of the waters below.

The house's troubled seasons had finally come to an end. It had held on for longer than it should have, longer than it had life left in it. Its few slices of an American life that had been worth living became a part of its storied history, and what remained were fragments that could never again be restored. And as the house continued to crumble, I thought I heard the slight murmur of a voice I would never forget, as it had become a part of my very own.

When I returned to The Harboring, I climbed the stairs and lifted the shades and opened wide all the windows. I walked to the elongated kitchen counter and made certain that all the plastic dollhouse babies had been put to sleep in their plastic dollhouse cribs in their parents' colorful metal dollhouse, replete with flowered wallpaper, furniture, a fully-stocked refrigerator, miniature curtains at each window, patio furniture, miniature pictures on the walls of flowers and mountains and the sea, and one pink nursery and one blue nursery, and flower pots and hedges all around. Hanging from fishing line throughout the dollhouse were an array of vintage Cracker Jack toys, each one dangling from the ceilings of every room, like brightly-colored Christmas ornaments.

I stepped back and said with renewed finality the only words that could propel me to move forward with the last remaining act of both a desperate and anticipatory reunion with the one I had left behind. And the words that would save me came again, as if they had never left: "I did it."

I made a final ascent and climbed to the third floor, opened the door that led to the terrace that had never been used, and with arms outstretched, plummeted to the clear, hard surface below, thinking only that I had done what I had set out to do for someone who couldn't do it for themselves and for the one person who mattered most—who finally mattered most—myself. And somewhere on the way down, for the very briefest of moments, I saw what I had hoped to see all along: wide open spaces that just might have a place ready for me at the table where countless others just like me resided.

Epilogue

"Stop!"

"What?

"Stop! Shut off the engine," Mick Collins shouted, holding up his hand like a regimented school crossing guard.

Before shutting off the bulldozer's engine, Bill Collins reversed it back onto Crow Creek Road. He exited the heavy piece of machinery, just as his brother, Mick, held up his hand again and stood stock-still, looking very much like a deer in headlights, which was something everyone who had ever driven Route 16 had seen more times than they wanted to see, anticipating the appearance of the agile animal at every curve.

"What's up, Mick?"

"Uh, I'm not sure, but I need you to come a little closer to see if you see what I think I see."

As Bill approached, he said, "What the hell is that odor?"

Mick only continued to stand frozen in place, shaking his head, finally saying, "I could guess, but I don't want to."

Bill wiped both hands along the sides of his grease-stained navy work pants, then ran them both through his hair before sliding them into the pockets of his pants. "Holy shit," Bill said in a voice whose tremble surprised even him. "Mick, what the hell?"

"I know. Jesus help us," Mick said with a tremble that matched his brother's.

The two men put one heavy boot foot in front of the other, as they approached the nearly demolished house. "Is that..."

"No, it can't be."

Mick and Bill Collins had grown up in Fayette County, married sisters, and brought up more than a few fine children who were growing into even finer adults, near replicas of their parents. To some, their stories would seem not only uneventful, but mundane; and yet, their respective stories were filled with fortitude and perseverance; disappointments, placed in the grand scheme of things; losses that were recovered without much fanfare. So, to an equal amount, their stories were envied by more than a few, especially as life ran its course and the end approached and one either reveled in it or regretted it. And the latter was not welcomed by any.

The Collins' stories were composed of moments that would not make a news story or be recorded in any records save for birth and death and a few seemingly insignificant moments throughout; and yet, they were each stories that everyone, deep down, yearned to live. Living a simple life was so deeply embedded in the Collins families that to live anything else would have never occurred to any of them. It was as lovely as it sounds, as lovely as they lived it.

As the two brothers approached, Mick had already pulled from his jacket pocket his cell phone. As much as he wanted to believe that it was not his friend lying covered in a sheet of blood on a bed inside a house where they had all camped outside, roasted marshmallows over an open fire, and pulled from the waters mouth-watering trout, he knew that his friend's slight grin was a grin worn only by him. He also knew that his friend had endured more than enough and that with every fire started and every bed rolled and every pole immersed in the waters, he prayed to be set free from all that troubled him, knowing all along that the journey would never end.

He made the sign of the cross, as did Bill, before calling 911 to report what he himself could not believe; and yet, for just a slight moment in time, he knew his friend had been welcomed to the table. And that was more than enough.

> *What man of you, having a hundred sheep, if he has lost one*
> *of them, does not leave the ninety-nine in the open country,*
> *and go after the one that is lost, until he finds it? And when*
> *he has found it, he lays it on his shoulders, rejoicing...*
>
> — LUKE 15:4-5

Panchlora Nivea

A da Weevil tapped on the crusty shell of the cockroach with the tip of a black plastic-coated bobby pin that she kept an ample supply of in her back pocket. She used one on each side of her hair to hold in place the straight bangs that she was trying to grow back.

And as she bent to examine the cockroach, the bobby pin on the right side loosened and settled beside the cockroach. And until she picked it up to hold her bangs back in place, her vision was blocked in that eye temporarily, putting on hold for a few minutes the further examination of the specimen. She tried closing her right eye and relying only on her left eye. She found herself chuckling, even though she knew that what she was thinking was not funny.

She recalled a distant cousin who had a lazy eye and a mean disposition. She didn't want to be like him. "He's meaner than a snake," her pawpaw always said whenever anyone brought up his name, turning his head to the right and spitting a line of tobacco juice onto the front yard, his hunting dog, Daisy, jumping back a few feet every time.

Her mother was annoyed whenever Ada forgot to pull back the fallen strands with the bobby pins, but Ada didn't seem to mind the intrusion. She just dealt with it. Every time this happened, her mother would say, "Oh, for the love of Christ, Ada." Her mother didn't mind so much the growing-out stage, which was something Ada had decided to do more than once, but it was the bangs falling into her eyes that caused her mother irritation, like the itch from a bad rash. Ada never could figure out why this cycle bothered her mother. After all, she was the one who had to contend with the annoyance, and yet for Ada it wasn't really an annoyance. She liked to watch them fan out as she blew air upwards, the created wingspan somewhat humorous to her way of thinking. At other times, she liked to snap her head with enough fervor to send the growing bangs to the side, even though they remained there for only a brief moment before sliding back down. But this game she liked. And she would often chuckle at its cyclical nature. "Ada, would you please pull those bangs back with a bobby pin. You know how I hate it when they fall all over your eyes. Honestly, I don't know how you stand it." And Ada's mother would send from her mouth a cloudy stream of cigarette smoke, which Ada hated as much as her mother hated her bangs falling into her eyes.

She couldn't understand why her mother smoked one after the other, until she learned in health class that it was an addiction, like her father's alcohol. And one like her father's that would eventually leave an unhappy trail in its wake, like a feral cat. Ada knew this certain demise without reserve. And her mother knew it too, as she sat by the open window, a slightly moth-eaten throw wrapped around her shoulders like she was expecting the summer heat to change suddenly, readying herself for inclement weather. She knew better than to tell her mother what she thought every time she scolded her for something that seemed so unimportant.

To Ada's way of thinking, what did a few wild strands of hair mean next to world hunger and poverty and global warming and a mother addicted to nicotine and a father addicted to alcohol? What did it matter that she let her bangs grow out—again—and that unless she held them back with a bobby pin, the world would end if they fell into her eyes? She didn't know who would care or why, but apparently her mother did.

Naturally, Ada didn't vocalize any of these thoughts. She yearned to, but instead played them over and over in her head, which ended up bringing her a tremendous amount of satisfaction. Ada wanted desperately too to remind her mother of the dangers of cigarette smoking, but only repeated the litany silently, having bookmarked a page in her health textbook, checking off each one with a different colored pencil to keep the repetitive boredom at bay. She knew that her mother knew the dangers without being told, like her father, but their apparent denials said otherwise. She wondered about the perspective of it all.

The black, plastic-coated bobby pins were kept on her mother's dresser top inside a chipped China dish with painted, faded pink roses in the center, a honeybee etched inside the bud working at its nectar. Ada liked to move the pins to the sides of the dish to reveal the roses, but they always slid to the center, befriending the roses that were apparently embarrassed by their growing lack of appeal, like the pink fingernail polish that seemed to chip from Ada's fingernails before they even had time to completely dry because she was too impatient to wait.

Ada spotted the comatose cockroach as she left the library, nearly stepping on it, but seeing it just before the ball of her right foot started its descent, tripping over her flip-flops as her eyes met the legs of the insect, Dr. Grub catching her before she toppled him over, too.

"Whoa there, Miss Ada. What's your hurry?"

"Oh, Dr. Grub, I'm so very sorry. I was just about to squash the living daylights out of that cockroach there, which seems to be deader than a doorknob anyway, but you know how I just love bugs, even dead ones."

"Yes, young lady, I know you do. Well, carry on," and he set Ada back on solid ground, picking up the book her favorite librarian had suggested she read, because she knew how much Ada loved the life of bugs. And recalling now the opening sentence of *The Metamorphosis* seemed to lessen Ada's embarrassment just a bit.

"Thanks, Dr. Grub. Carry on."

Dr. Grub chuckled and winked, and Ada tried very hard to focus on the cockroach instead of Dr. Grub's lean frame and angular jawline and deep-set chocolate eyes, not to mention his perfectly pleated khaki trousers and his starched white cotton shirt with his monogram in navy blue block letters on the pocket, the cuffs turned inside each sleeve, not over the sleeve, like her daddy wore. And everything else about Dr. Grub reminded her of her daddy.

She didn't want it to, but it did. She imagined that her daddy might have seen himself in Dr. Grub, too. Ada closed her eyes, shook her head as if to clear her mind of any thought of her daddy, and crouched down to further inspect the insect. She didn't have time today to fantasize about Dr. Grub and her mother one day marrying and all of them living happily ever after, Dr. Grub convincing her mother to stop smoking cigarettes incessantly and return to her former self—the one in the photograph on top of Ada's second-hand dresser, her mother wearing a red, white, and blue cotton sailor blouse with three buttons designed to look like sailboats, her teeth sparkling white like piano keys, not the growing color of light rust, her hair clean and fresh and resting in waves on the tips of her shoulders.

She opened and straightened the black, plastic-coated, bobby pin—something else her mother would have scolded her for, since that meant the end of yet "another perfectly good bobby pin"—and poked gently at the legs of the cockroach, noticing that one of them was missing. She also noticed that this insect had only three legs, not six like the other cockroaches she kept. Another mysterious observance was that this cockroach was very pretty in color, unlike the other cockroaches that she had amassed in her collection. And suddenly, as if she had just been told that summer would last another month, her heart fluttered just a bit.

She realized that this specimen was a Cuban cockroach, something she had only seen pictures of in her insect field guild. She further examined its underbelly's intricate, transparent webbing, pulling out from the back pocket of her Levi's her small orange spiral notebook and skinny red pencil, trying to record if its various greens matched more the color of faded lawn grass or pistachio, her very favorite nut. The insect's coloring was completely different from the reddish-brown shading of all the other cockroaches she had seen before, which was very close to the recent auburn hair coloring that her mother had applied to her own tresses: Clairol's Balsam 612rb, medium reddish brown.

While the cockroaches that she had in her collection had the translucent webbing that reminded Ada of stockinged-faced burglars, this one reminded her of an intricate X-ray film that revealed layer upon layer of a delicate, flaky pastry with pistachio cream filling in between its multilayered construction. It also reminded her of a vintage photo negative that was tinted in a pale color of yellow, two couples posed, frozen in time; the ladies looking demure; the men, unabashed. Ada's daddy convinced her that the reason she loved pistachio nuts was because when her mother was pregnant with her, she craved them. Her daddy would shell them night after night for her mother for nine long months until he was convinced that he wore the shading of the nut on the tips of his fingers.

Ada looked and looked for the remnants of the shading whenever he took her hand on their walks through the woods behind their rural Appalachian home collecting butterflies and caterpillars and moths and beetles and ladybugs and melodious cicadas and crickets and grasshoppers. But even when she squinted and became nearly comatose from being fixated on his fingers, she could never see the color of pistachios.

"Oh, it's there," he said, whenever she insisted that she couldn't see it. "You're not looking close enough. Maybe one day when you are older, you will see it clearly," he would say in his gentle, almost whisper-like voice. But that was so long ago that Ada would find herself surprisingly in tears trying to recall those moments that, over time, had blurred—much like the negative she kept in an old cigar box, along with her dead insects and her collection of vintage Cracker Jack prizes, and the smallest bird nest she had ever seen.

When Ada flipped the insect over, she discovered overlaying, feather-like wings that, when lifted, were like looking through a slightly frosted window, on an early winter's morning. Ada found that without remembering when, she was no longer crouching over the bug, but eyeing it at ground level, oblivious to passersby entering and exiting the library. She lifted the bug from the concrete pavement and gently touched its slightly oily body.

A warm summer breeze, dripping from the sweltering humidity, picked up enough momentum to sweep Ada's bangs back like magic, setting to flutter ever so slightly the wings of the cockroach, and suddenly Ada wished it was alive and set free to fly.

Shuffle

Dewey Allan's head had fallen straight forward, his chin resting at the base of his neck, a few gray strands of his fine hair lightly touching his bushy eyebrows. The half-read newspaper mimicked his own resolve, resting limply on his knees, and once again his wife of nearly 50 years found herself recalling days when their energy level was much higher, and they were less prone to drop off to sleep mid-morning.

Fanny, rising from her old, nearly threadbare faded green floral upholstered chair to walk towards him, bended at the waist just a bit and leaned in slightly towards Dewey to check to make sure that he was, indeed, breathing gently, barely tapping his rounded shoulder before walking to the scratched cherry table that had sat at the front entry for more years than she could recall. She pulled open the drawer and reached underneath the stack of Kmart receipts and Kroger receipts and Walgreens receipts to recover the stack of cards that she had created and amassed over the past several months from watching segments of HGTV's *House Hunters*, the deck tied with a satin aubergine ribbon.

Fanny had created each card from sheets of multi-colored construction paper, using the ace of hearts from a deck of playing cards as a template, remembering now the child-like thrill she felt when she pushed her buggy down the aisle of school supplies, memories of shopping for pencils and notebooks and boxes of Crayola crayons for her children, who were now grown and married with children of their own traveling through her memory, like the steady trickle of water that constantly ran from their kitchen faucet. She recalled that initially it had been a rather silly idea, but now that the project was complete, she thought differently. *Fanny*, she had said to herself at the time, *you have lost your mind.* But since she began the project, she was convinced that it might have been a good idea after all. Perhaps one of her best ideas ever.

She recalled making the trip to Kmart several months ago when back-to-school promotions were underway, advertisements in the Sunday paper spilling from the center folds onto her dated red and white chrome kitchen table like leaves falling from the trees at the beginning of the fall season. Advertisements for jeans and shirts and athletic shoes and backpacks, and school supplies that ranged from the obvious to hand sanitizers and packs of Kleenex tissues blanketed the tabletop. Fanny observed the scattered sheets of colorful advertisements and recalled from her days of decoupaging that a light coating of adhesive just might improve the lackluster tabletop, covering up years of use, but suddenly dismissed the idea completely after realizing that she would always know what was underneath.

Fanny sighed and picked up the pile of advertisements and crushed them into the trash can underneath the kitchen sink. Now, she sat at that same kitchen table, rocking back and forth as the right back chair leg had lost its footed cap, causing it to wobble just a bit—not necessarily in an annoying way as much as in a rhythmic, somewhat therapeutic way, allowing Fanny time to replay in her mind the day last summer when she had made the trip to Kmart to pick up a new Barbie doll for her granddaughter's birthday, a pair of cotton flannel pajamas for herself, and a pack of Fruit-of-the-Loom undershirts for Dewey.

It was on hearing the excited voices of a group of children a few aisles over from her in the office supplies section of the store—right next to the outdoor barbecue grills—that caught her attention. And she found herself led to the cacophony of voices, guiding her buggy past shampoos and conditioners and toothbrushes and toothpastes and myriad analgesics, smiling at the children selecting neon-colored spiral notebooks and packs of mechanical pencils, before she found herself almost unknowingly pulling from the shelf the pack of multi-colored construction paper and a box of colored pencils and a pair of craft scissors and a bottle of Elmer's glue and a wooden ruler, throwing them into her cart with equal abandon. And before she knew it, she began to laugh uncontrollably, until the children all chimed in, unsure whether they were simply humoring an old lady or actually finding the whole experience as jovial as she found it. And in the end, it was irrelevant since either way brought Fanny a feeling of happiness and hopefulness and excitement that had remained an elusive visitor for longer than she was willing to admit.

She remembers pushing her buggy rather quickly to the checkout counter, glancing at her wristwatch to make sure that she would arrive home in time to make lunch, settling into the dip of her chair's seat, sipping an ice-cold bottle of Coca-Cola, and watching *House Hunters* at noon, Dewey shaking his head from side to side at her routine and smiling gently at the same time. She had grown to resent the head movement, finding it, like most of his repetitive bodily movements, both irritating and unnecessary, but still finding the grin endearing. And as incredulous as it might seem—and it certainly seemed so—it was still his sweet, gentle smile that continued to bring her the unmeasured joy not unlike the lingering feeling of waking to falling snow on Christmas morning. And while the cracking of his right thumb and the rising of his eyebrows and the restlessness of his legs in bed at night seemed to be more pronounced now than ever before, Fanny was certain that he was just as annoyed with her incessant lip-biting and fingernail cuticle trimming, even though she secretly hoped that he was not in the least bit annoyed by anything she did or said. This thought made her smile, even though she knew it was ridiculous to entertain.

When Fanny slipped from the open-ended pack of construction paper a golden yellow sheet, she smiled. Dewey's favorite color had always been yellow, and she found herself—without giving it any thought at all—selecting the golden yellow-colored sheet to start her project. And, looking over both shoulders to assure herself that she was alone, she brought the sheet of construction paper to her nose and inhaled. Suddenly, she was back in Miss Sally's art class as a first-grader, and she closed her eyes for a brief moment and smiled. With the precision she had once used in every task she tackled, from preparing meals to household chores to detailed costume designs for her children's holiday attire but that had diminished over the years since they had left home to start lives of their own, Fanny found herself humming Harry Chapin's "Cat's in the Cradle" as she laid down the ace of hearts, drawing from a mechanical pencil a speck of lead, and tracing around the playing card.

Taking the craft scissors from the heavy plastic wrapper and cutting out the 2 ½" x 3 ½" yellow card, she opened the box of colored pencils which, to her surprise and delight, had already been sharpened. She chose a Mediterranean blue colored pencil, because the couple from Fort Lauderdale, Florida, on today's episode of *House Hunters* had paired yellow and blue in their ocean-front condo. She wrote the date across the top of the card and a description of the condo and the view and the striped yellow and blue side drapery panels that flanked the two sets of French doors that led to the patio. Her rendition, while rather simple to create since it merely involved straight lines representing windows and doors, delighted her.

She held the card at arm's length and tried not to be pleased at what she had created. And yet, when she looked to her front picture window, she could easily see that it could work in her own small country cottage, the colors especially uplifting during the long frigid months of winter. And yet, the card needed more. She retrieved from the corner of the family room her knitting basket, pulling from it a shank of blue yarn and a shank of yellow yarn and clipped a small sample from each. She Scotch-taped the pieces of wool to the card and said, "Done," and set it aside.

Over the course of the next several months, Fanny rotated the brightly colored sheets of construction paper: yellow, purple, green, blue, pink, red, and even black. With every new episode, Fanny looked forward not only to the selection and design choices of the home buyers, but little by little found herself making changes to what the new homeowners chose. And little by little, Dewey began to watch with her, catching her completely off guard one day when he said, "I think they should choose house number three. It's the better investment."

Fanny stopped eating her toasted pimento cheese sandwich and looked at Dewey as if he had just risen from the dead and was walking across the Sea of Galilee. "What did you say, dear?"

"Oh, uh, nothing," and she grinned and turned her head so he wouldn't see it. Little by little, Fanny created one card after another, each with decorating ideas that she, in time, might try herself. Cards that had drawings of farm sinks, hardwood floors, paint colors, lighting fixtures, stainless steel refrigerators, walk-in showers, and a fireplace in the master bedroom. She became more and more adept at her artistic skills and more and more detailed, returning to Kmart to purchase little packs of multi-colored beads and gold filament thread and even splurging on a pack of dollhouse-sized wallpaper.

After several months and a few dozen cards had been created, Fanny discovered that a couple of cards were missing. She recalled a card that rearranged the placement of the living room furniture, after seeing an episode that had so intrigued her. It was the first time that she had actually changed something in her own house immediately after watching a show. Their once vibrant red leather sofa, while worn from years of use on the arm rests and at the back where Dewey often rested his head, was no longer flush against the wall. With the help of the young man who mowed their lawn, the sofa was brought out a few feet from the wall so that a pathway was created behind it—something a young Asian couple had dubbed feng shui, Fanny recalled. And while Dewey had simply shaken his head at the pronouncement and rearrangement, Fanny noticed that he had begun to walk around the back of the sofa in order to gaze out at the small pond outside their living room—something that he had seldom done before.

And she noticed, too, that he often stopped on his journey, resting for a bit as he leaned on the back of the sofa looking around the room in a way that she had never before seen him do. And whenever she played this scene over in her head, a certain delight came over her that she couldn't quite describe. And yet it made her happy to know that he had noticed that something was different. Fanny continued to look through the stack of cards and discovered that the first card that she had created—the one with the Mediterranean blue-and-yellow-striped drapery panels—was one of the cards that was missing.

She looked around her at the floor thinking that it may have slipped from underneath the aubergine ribbon and fallen, but she did not see it anywhere. Then she returned to the hall table drawer, removing all the sales receipts, but still nothing. It was then that she heard the sound of drilling, and walked slowly yet deliberately to the front of the house. Perched on the ladder above the picture window was the young man who mowed their lawn, installing drapery rods, Dewey shaking his head up and down in approval and grinning.

And Fanny quietly took her seat at the faded green floral uphol-stered chair, the dip of the seat offering familiarity and comfort, and watched Dewey, the missing card peeking out from inside his back trouser pocket.

Sylvie's Nature

Michigan Avenue meanders through the town, east to west, from the desecrated center of Coal Country, parallel to the still Kanawha River on its left; a lineup of pink, blossoming dogwoods on the right hides the rusted railroad tracks. And yet, the rocking sounds of the slow, once loaded, but now only partially filled rail cars can still be heard in a loud whisper if you lean in close. And we follow as if in a trance, the irregular, clickety-clack sound as the train's wheels roll over the rail joints.

Like most of us, these cars are tired; and yet, we still listen. We still find something more than a bit reassuring that while it may only be a speck of the familiar, it is still a speck. And for most of us, that is surprisingly enough. Sylvie Martin's travails are familiar to each of us, as our own journey mimics hers in ways that we can not only relate, but also in ways we can't relate to at all. While she, too, visits the sick at the long-term care center the next town over every Monday, reads aloud to the nursery school children on Wednesdays, and works part-time evening shifts at the only restaurant left in town, The China Buffet, it is her hour-long, weekly walk every Saturday morning through town, through Plum Creek Hollow, to the maximum-security prison that sits like a cherry on top of a hot-fudge sundae (although it's clearly anything but), that both separates and connects us one to the other.

Her walk begins at the far east end of town as she stops, squints, and fingers the remains of the red-stenciled name of the dance studio, the image of the faded, bubble-gum colored pointe shoe barely visible—except in her mind—trailing ribbons reduced to dashes. She pulls from the heavy camo print backpack slung over her left, stooped shoulder, a tissue and dabs at the corners of her puffed eyes, shakes her head of the disappearing vividness, and walks west. Her limp is pronounced, like an exclamation mark in motion. For as long as anyone can remember, Sylvie taught ballet to every little girl in the valley who dreamed of one day being a ballerina; in the end, it being only just that—a dream, but a dream, nonetheless.

She crosses the barren street and wedges a wilted daisy between the weathered driftwood that has been nailed to an oak tree's thick trunk. The canary yellow, crudely-written message has survived seasonal attacks: John 10:11, a childlike sketch of a white dove in flight carrying a barely-visible red heart in its mouth and three carved, brown crosses below it. She crosses back and continues her journey.

"Good morning," Elsie bellows from her opened kitchen window, as she wipes dry the dishes from the draining rack. Sylvie only lifts her chin in response, but Elsie knows that is all she has to give, and it is enough. As Sylvie makes her way through town, friend after friend offers a wave or a greeting, but nothing more, knowing that Sylvie's mind is intent on making her weekly journey to do nothing more than to sit with Billy and make small talk and perhaps laugh a bit, and, if they're very lucky, cry even less.

While some in this valley have barely avoided incarceration for criminal deeds such as possession of drugs, spousal abuse, embezzlement, and myriad other atrocities, Billy knew that after he carried his shotgun out of the house one frigid winter day last year that he would end up incarcerated for life. He had warned his son-in-law for the last time that if he ever hit his daughter again, he would kill him; and he did. He had discussed it with Sylvie as if they were discussing plans for their yearly visit to Myrtle Beach. It was that innocuous. Before he left to drive 15 minutes east of their home, Billy kissed Sylvie goodbye, and she hugged him close, knowing that nothing would ever be the same, embracing what was to come. And knowing that Billy had just been diagnosed with inoperable stomach cancer simply, to them, paved the way for what had to be done. They each accepted the inevitable outcome with the calm of a gentle wave that would take them both far out to sea, showing immense gratitude for such a timely gift.

Sylvie knows each abandoned house and business along Michigan Avenue: the ones facing foreclosure, the ones occupied by those waiting for a certain exit, and the ones with algae-covered, aboveground swimming pools nearing collapse, the children having long ago moved on to greener pastures—she hopes. It's a day covered with Mediterranean blue skies, white puffy clouds, and patches of sunlight slipping through. The butcher shop where bologna was cut thick from a gleaming white porcelain slicer and served on Betsy Ross white bread with lettuce, tomato, Longhorn cheese, mayonnaise, and a smile and a wink was now boarded up with plywood, the width no match for the all-beef staple. Coils of fresh Italian sausage lined the meat case, like garden snakes. And shouts of victory from a game of poker in the back room drifted on a breeze, out the door.

She smiles, recalling that Billy was often playing poker and that whenever she and Ellen stopped by Billy would wave and throw each one a kiss. Mongrels yawn in front of the fire department's one truck, gleaming in the late afternoon sun, with neither sound nor movement, just catatonic stares, as their gaze follows the lone resident making her way west along Michigan Avenue to the abandoned school yard, sans students, teachers, athletes, and fluffy, sparkly, pom poms held in the hands of bouncing cheerleaders. Weeds, overgrown brush, and scattered trash inhabit the ground that was once alive with revelers keeping crossed all appendages for a way out.

"Tell Billy to hang in there, Sylvie," Billy's childhood friend offers, each of them knowing that there is not much else he can do. Her neighbors have stopped asking if they can give her a ride up the hollow. This journey is a journey she must make for herself, her way, in retribution for a sin committed that she knows was a pure, certain choice. She whistles a tune from *Grease* and tugs at the waist of her black denim, ankle-length jeans, pulling down on the black, crew neck tee. She passes the only store in town that remains open for business— The Bible Book Store—and hurls first one pebble after another at its spalled brick exterior.

The store's owner, Maggie, stands at the window and gazes at her, until she doesn't. All that remains of DB's Furniture Store are three oak rocking chairs blocking the sidewalk, moving slightly with the warm air, and Sylvie stops for a minute, arrested by the wondering of the ghosts who remain in motion. The bright red-tiled, polished exterior of the Corner Thrift Store retains its spotless front window panes. She steps up to the front, sets her backpack on the ground at her feet, and pulls from it a frayed, fabric cosmetic case. She's as thin as a whippet. She applies a generous amount of cherry-red color to her cracked lips, presses them together, and emits a certain popping sound, adding a light chuckle. She looks up to the black, metal lattice strips at the top of the red-tiled building and brings the strands of her jet black tresses together, combing through each with her fingers. She reaches into the jeweled back pockets of her jeans and pulls a long, white, silk ribbon. She ties the ribbon first into a bow and then decides to just let the ends trail, after first knotting the ribbon. She steps back, looks at herself in the clear glass, and shrugs as if to say, "It's as good as it's gonna get." Her resolve is blinding.

A police cruiser passes with the slowness of Steinbeck's turtle crossing the road, brakes, nods in her direction, and moves west, more than confident that there is no imminent danger. She crosses the street, walks under the railroad trestle on a winding road that leads to the all-male, maximum-security prison. On her left is a crystal clear stream, with a forest of mountain laurel covering the hillside. The water skips over the carpet of pea gravel. She removes her flip-flops, wades across, and emits a near-reverent, "Ahhh." When she reaches the far side, she sits down on the barren ground and removes from her backpack a paper plate, a plastic fork and knife, a can of sardines, and a sleeve of saltines. Each of these she sets on top of a clean white cloth.

A tiny spider, a butterfly, and a praying mantis join her at a distance. She picks up a bird feather and a fallen acorn and puts them in the breast pocket of her tee shirt. She eats with intention, making the sign of the cross before eating the first bite. When she's thirsty, she cups her hands and gathers into them a taste of the clear, cool water, splashing some on her face and absorbing the splash with a fresh tissue. Satiated, she leans back on her backpack and closes her eyes for more than a few minutes. And then she rises, pirouettes, gathers unto her what is hers, and continues along her certain journey, her soiled, faded, frayed pointe shoes dangling from her backpack. Motorists who pass underneath the railroad trestle wave, without beeping their horns, knowing that Sylvie would not welcome much else, knowing that Sylvie is readying herself for the final leg of the journey.

Entering the hollow, Sylvie stops first at the post office—a simple, white-painted block structure where the American flag and a black and white POW/MIA flag sway gently with the warm morning breeze. She passes the meandering creek on her right and somehow feels as if her spirit has left her and joined the light ripples. She can identify nearly every family in every house she passes, stopping to pat the heads of the dogs that seem to know it's time for Sylvie. Even they know to keep the barking to a minimum. Once she passes Anderson's Boarding House, with its pretty, blossoming Bradford pear trees, she stops briefly to gaze at their beauty, admiring once again the symmetrical design of the two-story black-shuttered house with its second level, end-to-end porch that mirrors the one on the main level, her eyes traveling to the three dormers on the third floor.

As she approaches the final ascent to the prison where she will be reunited with Billy, the sun has emerged in full, its rays ricocheting off the heavy, steel, barbed wire of the fence that surrounds the facility. She knows that Nick, a high school friend, will be at the gate, and will, as much as he doesn't want to, put her through the same machinations that she is put through every week. And as he fights once again the tears that fall from the corners of his eyes, Sylvie will smile, Nick will stop crying, and she will be allowed to enter a space from which she has no desire to leave, knowing all along that every step on her way back to town will be more tortuous than ever, but knowing too that she will willingly make it every week until there is no longer any reason, until the skies open and welcome one of their own.

Morning Line

...both rider and horse were cast into a deep sleep.

— Psalm 76:6

My mother was unloading the dishwasher when the blindingly polished coat of a copper-colored mare galloped past the ground-to-rooftop windows of our glass-backed rear patio. Its coat was as shiny as newly minted pennies and reflected the bright afternoon sun, glistening like liquid metal. Its brushed mane seemed to wave hello and goodbye in rapid succession.

Knives, forks, and spoons clinked and clanked across the travertine-tiled floor, making a cacophony not unlike those made by a toddler playing with drumsticks, as the cutlery basket dropped from my mother's hand. The utensils scattered from one end of the kitchen to the other, finding refuge underneath cabinets and getting stuck in air vents, one fork's tines looking askew, trying to determine whether it was safer above or below what was happening a few feet away.

As the mare continued to gallop from one end of our house to the other, my mother stood frozen in place, the cutlery basket on its side at her feet. And then two words broke my reverie: "Holy shit!" That's what she said. I swear. And if hearing her say it once wasn't shocking enough, she said it again. "Holy shit!" It was the first time a horse had ever been spotted in the back yard of our house in this unincorporated, rural town that we had recently moved to from Chicago, and it was the first time that I had ever heard my mother cuss. I couldn't decide which incident was the more incredulous. I was still too stunned by each, my pencil having been dropped on top of my notebook without my knowing it, the galloping mare interrupting the conjugation of French verbs. I must remember to thank that handsome equine when I make her acquaintance.

My mother and I watched in stunned silence, our mouths agape at the wonder that strode by until she stopped, turned, and stared with equal incredulity at first me, then my mother, and finally back at me again, until she sauntered off through the trees, stopping briefly to trample through my mother's vegetable garden, crushing her tomatoes and cucumbers before stopping to take a nibble of leaf lettuce. And that's when my mother said it again, "Holy shit!" And my forehead made a loud thud as it met my partially conjugated list of verbs. I was surprised at the reckless abandon with which those two contrasting words seemed to put me in an unfamiliar but very comfortable trance. I didn't bother, nor did I care, for an explanation.

Before my father came home from work, my mother said that she would wait to tell him about the horse visit until after he had consumed a couple gin and tonics, had his dinner, and retreated to his desk to pay the bills. It was not uncommon for my mother to follow this evening routine. Until my father enjoyed his after-work libations and had eaten his fill of my mother's mustard-rubbed pork tenderloin, sweet white shoepeg corn, and homemade barbecue baked beans topped with juicy strips of bacon and finely chopped onions, he would merely be an ornament at our kitchen table. He and my mother shared pleasantries with one another, I think merely for my sake, but I knew that things were strained between them. I just didn't know what to do about it, and I assumed that responsibility without much thought, believing without reserve that I alone knew the answers. I fantasized about wrapping each one up in pretty paper tied with pretty ribbon and setting them on top of the breakfast plates, like treasured lagniappes.

My father never asked me about my day at school or if I had made any friends since moving here (I hadn't) or even noticed that my mother had recently cut my bangs too short or that I had had my ears pierced and was wearing my mother's pearl studs that she had worn on their wedding day. He simply sat at the table, drinking his gin and tonics and staring out the window, the fingers of his left hand tap, tap, tapping on top of the walnut table. We had just read Edgar Allan Poe's "The Tell-Tale Heart" in English class, and suddenly I became acutely aware of the tapping of his fingers which seemed to grow louder and louder and my mother's immobilized focus on my father, her eyes seeming to bore straight through his body. I shivered, even through the heavy blanket of Appalachian heat and humidity that we wore like a second skin this time of year.

After I went to bed that evening, I heard the rise of my parents' voices which wasn't unusual, just unwelcomed. It, too, was routine. Come to think of it, most of what we did every day was as routine as the daily recitation of French verb tenses. And just as routine was my natural tendency to rise as if in a trance, slide quietly across the polished oak floors that wore my cotton ankle socks like a glove, until I reached the living room and came to an abrupt halt at the high pile of the grass green carpet that my mother forbade anyone to walk upon with shoes that had been worn outside. I mounted the top of the back of the raspberry-colored velvet Milo Baughman-styled sofa and grabbed hold of the soffit's edge, whose overhead exposed beams gave me a front-row seat of sorts to everything unfolding in the family room between my mother and my father. And something was always unfolding between them. The stage set was not elaborate, but extraordinarily ordinary, as if from a carefully choreographed Broadway performance and as certain as my own daily routine.

"I'm telling you, Stephen, just as I was about to put the cutlery in the drawer a horse ran back and forth across our patio from one end to the other, then proceeded to trample the garden and feast on my leaf lettuce. Thank God she didn't attack the rose bushes. I know it sounds crazy, but it happened. Ask Liv, if you don't believe me, which you never do. She'll tell you. A horse. I swear to God. A full-grown horse. It could have been a triple crown winner at the Belmont. It was that beautiful. The shiniest coat I have ever seen. Liv said that it reminded her of newly minted copper pennies. And such an air of confidence about it, too. Like it wasn't afraid of anything. Real strength. And a physical presence undeniably masculine. All it needed was a garland of deep red roses encircling its muscular steed and a confident, straight-backed jockey holding its reins in majestic and proud splendor. Certain, not ambiguous. It was, quite simply, the most arrestingly beautiful animal—thing—I have ever seen. Stunning, in a way that no jewel could compare, not even a perfect canary diamond which, by the way, you keep conveniently forgetting I want."

"First of all, Lois, it's Olivia, not Liv. You know how I hate it when you call her Liv. She, Olivia, would agree with you if you said there were monkeys hanging from the dogwood trees in our backyard. And second, nobody in this town owns a horse. We don't live out in the country, for Christ's sake."

"No," my mother interjected with a fierceness to her voice that frightened me just a bit, "we don't. Instead, we live out in the middle of nowhere. I would have much preferred the country to these hinterlands you brought us to. Oh, how you made us believe that we were moving to Nirvana when you brought us to this godforsaken place, with very little to do but look out the window every day, until it is nearly driving me nuts. Liv, too."

"Before you so rudely interrupted me, Lois, I was going to make my final point that if I've told you once I've told you a thousand times, that perfect canary diamond that you bug me for over and over is about as likely to surface on your finger as...well, as likely to happen as your seeing a horse gallop through your vegetable garden. Why in the world you want a canary diamond is beyond me. Oh, wait, I forgot, your father gave one to you on your sixteenth birthday, and you lost it in the Atlantic Ocean. Right. And one more thing, Oliva is perfectly fine." And my father snorted out his nose, a droplet just resting at its tip, until he wiped it away with his shirtsleeve.

"If my father was still alive, you wouldn't..."

"I am not your father, Lois," my father bellowed.

"No, you're not," I mouthed on the heels of his emphatic declaration, balling up my right hand and tapping with ferocity the wooden ledge.

"You are finally right about something! You will never be the man my father was—never. And make no mistake about it; Liv is not perfectly fine. Just saying the words doesn't make them true." My mother then lowered her head, removed her eyeglasses, and rubbed at the bridge of her nose.

All I wished was that she wouldn't cry. Seeing my mother cry, which she did with unnerving frequency, always, always made me sad to the point where I retreated to my bedroom, closed the door, and played Led Zeppelin's "Whole Lotta Love" over and over and over again until I felt better. And suddenly, it was getting harder and harder to hold on to the narrow wooden ledge that overlooked parents who had reached their saturation points, which was all too familiar to them and to me, sitting in a family room that was anything but. When I returned to my room, I wondered if I was fine or not, but before I could answer that question, I had drifted off to sleep to the hushed sounds of a house that seemed vacant.

93

I should have taken a picture of that horse, because a week after watching her gallop past our window, she hasn't reappeared. I just didn't think. I mean, it's not every day that a full-grown mare prances past your very eyes. At least not here, not in this town. Every day I come home from school, I rush into the house and ask my mother, "Did it come back? Did you see it?" And every day, she says, "Nope. Hasn't come back. But it will. I know it will. Don't you think so, Liv?"

I didn't answer that question. I want it to come back so that my mother would not think that she saw something that wasn't there. Here's what I said instead: "Why don't we ask around town and see if anyone has seen it or if anyone around here owns a horse?" I have asked this question before, and the answer is always the same, and it is just a little bit unsettling: "Liv, we have discussed the reason why we can't do that many times. If there is no horse in town and we start asking people if there is a horse in town, they will think that we are crazy, seeing a horse galloping through our back yard. Maybe we just thought we saw a handsome mare stride past our window and trample my garden."

"But Mom, I saw it, too. It was there in broad daylight. It was not a figment of our imaginations. It simply wasn't."

"Sweet Liv. Sweet, sweet Liv. Why don't you take your snack and go to your room and listen to your music? Was school okay today? Did you do well on your, what was it, your French test? It was today, wasn't it?"

"Yes, Mom," I said with a flatness to my voice that brought sadness for reasons with which I was all too familiar. I picked up the plate with a slice from my mother's crusty, thinly-sliced cranberry, walnut pumpernickel batard and cubes of Longhorn cheddar cheese with one hand and an opened, ice-cold bottle of Coca-Cola with the other, stopping briefly to first look at my mother whose smile was a bit uncertain, as she curled the ends of her blonde tresses around her finger, staring out the window, looking for something that would never again appear.

As I walked down the hallway to my room, I heard the faint whimper of my mother's cry as she began her routine to welcome home my father.

Pink Gingham Bows

We loved her in ways we shouldn't have, and she knew it, which made her love us in ways she shouldn't have, which caused all the problems—problems that none of us could have anticipated and yet each of us, in our hearts, knew possible. It was very much like the gathering of a storm. But we were drawn to her, and she was drawn to us like ants to sugar, and even if either of us had chosen to put blinders on like horses at a racetrack, the pull was stronger than either of us could resist. But like she always said, "Erase the word 'should' from your vocabulary and see what happens."

And like the dutiful and vulnerable students we were, we obeyed, like a fresh litter of gentle but very hungry puppies. We each knew—everyone, in fact, knew—that this mutual attraction would lead to nothing redeeming—it would, instead, lead to an eventual devastation that would leave us all in shards, as cutting as fine crystals of glass. And while it might have very well begun innocently enough, as time went on and we became nervously aware of its potential danger, we kept on doing it, as if we had suddenly turned into well-oiled automatons. We took turns adding to it a smidgen here and there, like a shopping list for the delectable fare to be offered at a dinner party. And once it picked up momentum, we couldn't stop it. It took on an intoxicating life of its own. And we really didn't want to stop it. But in our sub-consciousness, we knew that we should stop it. She knew it, too. And, looking back, there was no effort made to stop it.

And there it was again, that same word that kept resurfacing, that kept getting tossed to the side, as if a mere crumb from a crusty piece of French bread. There was no eliminating it; it kept reappearing, like a fine coating of coal dust after an overloaded coal truck passed by the lineup of houses in this stagnant Appalachian town. She didn't think the word "should" should have ever been invented in the first place. She often quoted a line from F. Scott Fitzgerald's *The Great Gatsby* in trying to explain to us why the word was pointless: "If you want to use the word, all you will end up doing is 'beat[ing] on, boats against the current, borne back ceaselessly into the past.'"

She detested the past, unless of course it pertained to American literary classics. And she was right about Fitzgerald's reference, as it applied to the mutual, growing attraction of each of us to the other. But then she was right about everything, until the day she was wrong, and so were we. It was a day that awakened in each of us the awareness as to just how wrong we had all been from the very beginning. But until that moment was birthed, we had the time of our lives.

Every student entering the junior class of 30 students that year at our small, private school noticed her the day she walked into the building for the first time as our new English teacher. Up to that point, none of us—not a single one of us—had ever liked our English teacher. Unyielding, structured, and as dry as toast were just a few of the chosen monikers we hung around their necks like wilted daisy chains.

We had all attended Cliff Top Montessori and St. Joseph's Elementary School. We had been together since the first grade, and we may as well have been living together in one big farmhouse on the outside of town, surrounded by acre after acre of lush woodlands, our parents practically living together in near-Bohemian style as it was, making sure that we received the best education their respective parents' money could buy, which they convinced themselves they had accomplished, bringing to each of us opportunities and experiences that we never, in our innocent youths, dreamed possible. And yet, the common thread that bound us one to the other was the single wall in each of our bedrooms that truly belonged to us to create song lyrics and Jackson Pollock-like art and poetry, and stories. And now, many years later, as we have all moved to the far corners of the world, that is the one gift that we chose to pass on to our own progeny.

We seldom reconnect, afraid that if reunited we could somehow bring her back, but separately, we're safe, having grown smart enough to stay clear of her intoxicating presence. And in retrospect, completely disengaging from one another was probably the best thing that could have happened to any of us, including her. She was that influential in our lives, and also, in the end, that destructive. Even our parents, in their deepest, darkest, most private moments had to admit that it all went wrong. And it would be something that would remain with us forever, both a curse and a blessing; a curse that hadn't yet and probably never would be lifted, maybe even one we didn't want lifted, like living with it was both a cloak and a dagger, all at the same time—something that we wanted to let loose, but something that we kept holding onto tighter every time we felt our hold relax.

Emily and I noticed it at the same time: that slender, pale pink gingham flat bow that she wore in her hair, parted slightly off center on the left side, a few wisps of straight-cut bangs lightly touching the tops of her eyebrows, her honey-colored bob emitting what seemed like rays of light, nearly blinding. The child-like bangs were cut as precise as an edge of notebook paper. Why we loved her without reserve was a mystery. A mystery then and still a mystery over 20 years later, after having graduated college, married (and divorced), with high school-aged broods of our own.

Our small Catholic high school was the only one in this rural area of Appalachia. We flew on the wings of our coal barren grandparents, who scooped up their own offspring to navigate their own paths. We drove BMWs and Hummers, and we came out miraculously unscathed by the crashes that came in waves from drunken stupors. The girls carried Louis Vuitton monogram canvas Speedy 35 satchels, and all of us wore nothing but Ralph Lauren when we escaped from the confines of our nondescript school uniform of navy cords, navy cotton skirts, and white Oxford cloth buttoned-down collared shirts. Denied anything that would identify us individually from 8:00 a.m. until 3:00 p.m. five days a week left us to make lifelong friends with Clairee Belcher from *Steel Magnolias*, her words ricocheting off the concrete walls of our school's hallways and classrooms: "The only thing that separates us from the animals is our ability to accessorize."

But she—our new, enigmatic English teacher—shared none of our materialistic commonalities, which simply added to her mysterious, intoxicating, inexplicable pull. She wore Birkenstocks with a pair of ankle socks every day. The socks were never the same, and not a single one of us owned a pair of ankle socks. The thought never occurred to us to even consider ankle socks. Hers had everything stitched on them from baby chicks to paintbrushes, peace symbols and evergreen trees to mushrooms.

"How in the hell can we be so enamored by ankle socks?" Anna exclaimed one day at lunch.

"Ya got me," we chimed in unison.

"She's both sophisticated and yet very childlike," Chris observed, as he tossed a handful of peanut M&Ms into his open mouth, which is what he ate every single day for lunch.

Much to our approval, she never wore what we called "teacher jumpers." Instead, her wardrobe was entirely from a line called Blue Fish. She added to her lineup every summer from a shop in Soho and one in Charleston, South Carolina. The fact that she spent summers in New York City (where every single one of us wanted to land) and the winter breaks in South Carolina simply added to the allure of these free-flowing, tunic-style dresses made from organic cotton and linen, hand-painted with daises, insects, and yes, fish of every kind. Each piece touched just the tip of her ankle socks, and she wore them with such confidence that we secretly wanted to sneak into her closet and play dress-up, knowing perfectly well that we could never pull it off.

She lived two blocks from the school, and as we sat at our desks every morning (although she often let Liam sit on the floor because he wanted to and allowed Graham to perch on the back of his desk, again, because he wanted to) before class started, we watched her round the corner with a hurried step because she was always late, abhorring mornings as much as we did, her damp tresses catching the early-morning breeze, her brown leather crossbody bag swinging to the sounds of the church bells. She was Audrey Hepburn running through the streets of Rome in *Roman Holiday*.

The summer before our senior year, a few of us traveled with her to New York City, where she had chosen to wake early one morning and quietly steal away from our rooms at The Plaza to John Barrett's Salon in Bergdorf-Goodman across the street. She left a note for us to order breakfast. When she returned, her bob had been dyed a color very close to orange sherbet. We bellowed with approval. She simply shrugged her shoulders, opened wide her arms, and gathered us in like too many inflatable parrots won at a game along the state fair midway. And even though we were more than a bit surprised that she didn't discuss this decision with us beforehand—for while she talked about sentence structure and the components of a well-written essay and her undying love for the classics, she talked with us most assuredly about life—we were instantly struck dumb by her unilateral decision.

Instead of voicing our disapproval, we accepted her embrace by enveloping her too into a gentle, but firm grasp and taking turns planting long-awaited kisses on her fair cheeks. And, in looking back, perhaps that was the denouement that changed the course so very much. That and a flat, cotton, pink gingham bow that invited more than any of us could have ever imagined. It was both magical and threatening.

After the start of the new school year, we drove by her apartment one evening to pick her up for dinner and a movie—something that happened with greater frequency than it should have happened. As she descended the stairs from the front entrance of her building, Erica said, "If she wasn't so damn cute, I'd have to hate her. But look at her, she's just fucking cute!" And we all agreed.

By spring, she had grown quite ill. One early morning, after announcements, her students were gathered in the library, as she announced that she would be resigning, as a hush and a stillness drew everyone to a quiet center that was unwelcomed, unfamiliar, and unsettling. And while our little community mourned her departure, upon reflection many years later, it was her style to leave with quiet exactitude and dignity. Anything else would have disappointed us. And while she wanted to stay and stay forever, she couldn't. She would never jeopardize her students' acquisition of knowledge or bear their witness as she fell into an eventual decline in body and in spirit, fearful of taking them along for the ride.

But perhaps the single most important reason for her withdrawal was her determination to avoid the early theft of childlike innocence that was still very much a part of each one of her students and a part of herself. After all, she had instilled in us a beauty that, while assured to fade over time, just might linger, just might prevail—a complete belief that anything is possible. For in the end, what became undeniable to everyone was that she too loved us in ways she shouldn't have. It was rumored (again, never confirmed) that she was on the verge of a nervous breakdown—too many losses in too short a time.

Her recent engagement to our theology teacher, Miss Brown, had been broken, her parents had been killed in a skiing accident, and her only sibling had committed suicide, leaving a note for her that she read and set fire to on the rooftop garden terrace of her apartment building, from where the building super escorted her, until the fire had been extinguished, knowing that it was the one thing he could do to offer her some measure of peace. It was rumored that he had been in love with her and that she knew it but could not reciprocate his affections.

We knew we shouldn't have yearned to know the contents of that letter, but ashamedly we did. And as I remember her steadfast resolve and her resilience, and her insistence on the truth, the singsong melody of the birds in the trees above makes me giggle like a child, recalling the day we helped her sneak three arrestingly beautiful finches into her no-pets-allowed studio apartment. The apartment was so sparsely furnished that we wondered if she was planning to move, but we said nothing. We were just happy to be there.

There was a single bed dressed in the most luxurious of white Egyptian cotton sheeting, with a few standard-sized pillows and a European-sized pillow, and a single boudoir pillow, each covered with the same Egyptian cotton fabric, her initials in a deep salmon thread in the center. At the foot of the bed sat a simple, four-legged, flat-top writing desk with a simple, slender, brass-like lamp topped with an eggshell-colored linen shade. There was an easel that held each month's calendar, with the month etched in gold-tone lettering. Writing implements of every kind were housed inside a floral, decoupaged vessel, and a stack of leather-bound Smythson journals placed with intention in the center. The table was painted the color of bright green Easter basket straw grass. At the base of the journals were the texts we used for our creative writing class: Brenda Ueland's *If You Want to Write* and Anne Lamott's *Bird by Bird*.

The Shaker-styled, straight-backed, birch wood desk chair looked rigid, uncomfortable, and yet perhaps so very necessary to penning journal entries that gifted clarity, but not until the harsh realities of life's difficult adventures were revealed first. Two flamingo-pink leather nail-head trimmed chairs sat at the far end of the room, a luxurious Stark floral carpet anchoring it all. It was both fairy-like and devoid of anything that would identify its inhabitant. And suddenly, we realized we didn't really know her at all; only what she chose to show and tell, like a game learned in nursery school.

After we set up the elaborate Victorian-styled bird cage and lifted the front latch and released each finch into its newest confines, pressing inward on what looked like exact replicas of paper takeout containers from a Chinese restaurant, we added a few bird toys for their amusement and left, without a word. She had named the finches after the characters from her favorite novel, *To Kill a Mockingbird*: Atticus, Boo, and Scout, and we coveted each one of those, too. And what remained in the end was the challenge to each of us to live life, to simply and with fevered abandon, live life.

Needle's Eye

Astra inclinant, sed non obligant.
"The stars incline us, they do not bind us."

Abby woke up on Monday morning; it could very well have been any other morning of the week, for one mirrored the others. She couldn't recall when one had last differed from the others. She was certain that they had each been different, but she simply couldn't recall the last time she recognized the differences.

But this morning, she reached for her iPhone to set the alarm for 11:32 p.m. She had been planning this moment since she read a news article that alerted her again, over her iPhone, that the first pink supermoon of the year would be visible "at around 11:32 p.m." After over a year of suffering the ravages of COVID-19, her spirits were lifted at this refreshing news. She looked in her phone's reverse camera lens and wondered if the deep purple bruise on her left cheek had lessened to a shade of pink that it usually wore as it healed. She wondered how close to the supermoon's shade it would match. And catching her completely unaware, she saw a glimmer of a grin appear in the lens.

The pink supermoon would be larger than a full moon, and Abby yearned for the day to pass quickly, knowing that it wouldn't, because they never did. She parted her black and white patterned café curtains at her bedroom window, revealing a morning much too bright for her irritated eyes and a headache that was intense to an indescribable degree. And yet, she was energized, knowing that what she had planned, imagined, for so long, would happen on a day that months ago she didn't even know existed. Abby opened the door to her bedroom, knowing, like a teenager slipping out at night to meet her boyfriend, exactly how far to open the door before the hinge would squeak. She would peek around the frame to the front hall table to make certain that neither his keys nor his wallet were set inside the hunter green, caviar leathered tray. If they were still there, she would close the door and tiptoe back to her bed. If they were gone, she knew he was gone, too. She surprised herself every time at the immense exhale that was released.

She spent the mornings making certain that she had vacuumed the carpet in the direction he insisted on, dusted the tops of tables and chair legs, unloaded the dishwasher, and cleaned the bathroom until every surface gleamed bright. She made certain too that every towel—bath, hand, or kitchen—on every bar was centered, with ends even, one to the other. Abby was grateful that the apartment was small, with only two bedrooms, a living space, a shoe-box kitchen, and an equally small bathroom. A few years ago, Abby had forgotten to line up bottles of water on the countertop beside the refrigerator, but she didn't make that mistake again. Like all of them, it had been a costly one.

Blane's space was spartan: a gray leather sofa, two emerald green leather chairs, two black-coated metal floor lamps, a television set on top of a liquor cabinet, and a black vinyl-topped card table with two black metal folding chairs, where he sat for hours every evening putting jigsaw puzzles together while watching predictable action movies. Abby retreated to her bedroom every evening, just as she heard his door key inserted in the lock. She played a game with herself that she could reach her room before he even saw her. Most nights she succeeded. Once there, she settled herself—most times—

into a worn, but comfortable chair that was upholstered in a bold and colorful print of every imaginable shade of green. Flower stems and scattered leaves and budded tree branches intertwined among ornate, blue Chinese vases. The nail-head trim glistened from the flicker of a candle's flame that Abby lit every night, the scent of grapefruit wafting into every crevice of the room.

Abby looked at the carpeted floor often and snickered at its haphazard lines from intentional vacuuming. On the walls were original paintings that had belonged to her mother. They brought both comfort and distress for what she had once had but lost, and what she would never have again. And yet, she coveted them in a near-hedonistic way. An over-sized oil painting of the Lowcountry in vibrant hues found only in a fresh box of Crayola crayons was perched on the back top of her tiger's eye maple mule chest. A coastal scene with a lineup of sailboats ready to set sail was on the wall to the left of the upholstered chair. And placed next to the left side of her window—across from her bed—was a nude portrait of an expectant mother, lounging on an olive-green chaise, her pajama-clad toddler making every attempt to climb what to him was a growing mound that seemed insurmountable.

A small, grass-green-painted, simple writing table sat at the foot of the bed without a chair. Abby never used it except to admire its polished top and her collection of seashells gathered from times that, over the years, had faded in her memory. As she looked to each one, she liked that she could recall each one's different origins: triton and murex, cowrie, tulip and star, natica and tun. Scallops and small conchs though were her favorite.

Abby jumped when her iPhone's alarm sounded. What had she done all day? She remembered falling asleep in her chair in her room just after a lunch of leftover spaghetti and a piece of sea-salted dark chocolate. She remembered drifting off again and waking to the sound of Blane's key in the lock, and deciding to wrap her aubergine cashmere throw closer to her, but when had the sun disappeared? She quickly silenced her alarm, even though she knew that Blane would be in a deep sleep by now. But she didn't want to take any chances. Her worn brown leather Longchamp weekender was packed with the barest of essentials, nothing extra. She unzipped the bag to check again that the three small jewelry boxes were secure on the top of her carefully folded belongings. One container held her wedding rings, the other a three-inch high bisque cupid with an arrow sitting on a heart-shaped cushion that adorned her wedding cake. The last box housed a bright yellow glass chick figurine no bigger than a thumbprint that her mother carried in a little purse to church with her every Sunday when she was a little girl.

Abby planned to drive Midland Trail along Route 60, windows down in her aged BMW, listening to the waters of the New and Gauley Rivers, as the moon's light skipped over its reflection. She had traveled that road countless times. She wouldn't stop until she reached Hawks Nest Park Overlook, where she would walk the trail, remove her wedding rings from the box and toss them, one by one, over the cliff's edge, to the ravine below. She would return to her car and head the direction the winds pulled.

As she looked to the pink supermoon, hoping to not be disappointed, she blinked several times. It wasn't pink at all, not even a hint of pink. And it wasn't even golden in color, as the news reported. As the tears descended, Abby brought the curtain panels together, and the sounds from a rusted door hinge were faint, but deafening. Before turning away from the window, Abby glanced one last time at the night sky. As she squinted into the fullest moon that she'd ever seen, she saw, for the briefest of moments, a tinge of pink, even though she knew very well that, scientifically, the color pink did not exist.

"Don't worry," the voice whispered, "the second one is coming next month, same day," and the door's latch clicked closed.

Acknowledgments

The stringing of words into sentences and paragraphs that matter cannot see the full light of day without a team of objective, professional, dedicated lovers of the 26 letters of the alphabet, of a story that helps us make sense of the world around us. This gathered team enables the writer to reach levels that they would not otherwise reach.

Thank you to Ella Morgan Dillon, owner of Mountain Mama Book Reviews, for your close reading and critical analysis. You bring a most flavorful feast to the table every single time.

Thank you to my friend and discerning reader, Debbie Wells, for your valuable feedback on "The Harboring."

Caroline Carlson and Adam Giorgi first published six of these stories in The Daily Yonder; I remain honored and grateful for your support.

Thank you to the voracious readers who support my work, to the librarians who make a place for my books on their shelves, and to the countless booksellers who introduce readers to my stories.

Thank you to my publisher, Janie Jessee, and the staff at Jan-Carol Publishing for continuing to believe in my work.

In the end, though (always in the end), my most sincere gratitude goes to my husband, John, who has always encouraged me to put pen to paper (even when I was certain that the well had gone dry) and tell yet one more story. I could not do what I do without your support, nor would I want to.

About the Author

Kathleen M. Jacobs is an award-winning, critically acclaimed author of books for young readers, including *Honeysuckle Holiday*. She has also authored books of poetry and is a frequent contributor of commentary for a number of newspapers across the country. Her work has been published in literary journals and magazines, including *The Writer* and *Writer's Digest*. She has twice been chosen Runner-up Best Author of WV. She is a former English teacher on the high school and college levels and holds an MA in Humanistic Studies. She can be reached at www.kathleenmjacobs.com and on IG @kathleenm.jacobs.